A REDBIRD CHRISTMAS

A tale of enchantment and miracles at Christmas . . . Oswald T. Campbell, aged fifty-two, down-and-out in a Chicago winter, is given only months to live unless he moves South. He finds himself in the small town of Lost River, Alabama, where the residents are friendly if feud-prone and eccentric. One of them, Roy, keeps a red cardinal, a once wounded bird called Jack, in the village store. Patsy, a crippled little kid from a nearby trailer park, falls in love with Jack. What follows is an emotional roller-coaster ride through the lives of an engaging crew of misfits, fixers and ordinary good-hearted folk, set against the natural backdrop of a mellow Alabama winter, along the riverside.

FANNIE FLAGG

◆

A
REDBIRD
CHRISTMAS

Complete and Unabridged

CHARNWOOD
Leicester

First published in Great Britain in 2004 by
Chatto & Windus
The Random House Group Limited
London

First Charnwood Edition
published 2005
by arrangement with
Chatto & Windus
The Random House Group Limited
London

The moral right of the author has been asserted

British Library CIP Data

Flagg, Fannie
A redbird christmas.—Large print ed.—
Charnwood library series
1. Alienation (Social psychology)—Fiction
2. Alabama—Fiction 3. Christmas stories
4. Large type books
I. Title
813.5'4 [F]

ISBN 1–84617–002–8

Published by
F. A. Thorpe (Publishing)
Anstey, Leicestershire

Set by Words & Graphics Ltd.
Anstey, Leicestershire
Printed and bound in Great Britain by
T. J. International Ltd., Padstow, Cornwall

This book is printed on acid-free paper

FOR JONI, KATE, AND RITA

The Windy City

It was only November sixth but Chicago had just been hit with its second big blizzard of the season, and Mr. Oswald T. Campbell guessed he had stepped in every ice-cold ankle-deep puddle of dirty white slush it was possible to step in, trying to get to his appointment. When he finally arrived, he had used up every cussword in his rather large vocabulary of cusswords, owed in part to his short stint in the army. He was greeted by the receptionist and handed a clipboard.

'We received all your medical records and insurance forms, Mr. Campbell, but Dr. Obecheck likes to have a short personal history of his new patients, so could you please fill this out for us?'

Oh, God, he thought, why do they always make you fill something out? But he nodded cordially and sat down and started.

Name: *Oswald T. Campbell*
Address: *Hotel De Soto, 1428 Lennon Avenue, Chicago, IL*
Sex: *Male*
Age: *52*
Hair: *Some . . . Red*
Eyes: *Blue*

1

Height: *Five feet eight*
Weight: *161 pounds*
Marital status: *Divorced*
Children: *No, thank God.*
Closest living relative: *Ex-wife, Mrs. Helen Gwinn, 1457 Hope Street, Lake Forest, IL*

Please list your complaints below:

The Cubs need a new second baseman.

There were many more questions to fill out, but he just left them blank, signed his name, and handed it back to the girl.

★   ★   ★

Later, after his examination was over, as he sat shivering in a freezing room wearing nothing but a backless thin gray cotton gown, a nurse told him to get dressed; the doctor would meet him back in his office. Not only was he chilled to the bone and sore from just having been probed and prodded in many rude places, but now, to make matters worse, when he tried to put his shoes and socks back on they were still ice cold and sopping wet. He tried to wring the excess water out of his socks and managed to drip dye all over the floor. It was then he noticed that the dye from his socks had stained his feet a nice dark blue. 'Oh, great!' he muttered to himself. He threw the socks in the trash basket and squished down the hall in cold wet leather shoes.

As he sat in the office waiting, he was bored

2

and uncomfortable. There was nothing to read and he couldn't smoke because he had lied to the doctor and told him he had given it up. He wiggled his toes, trying to get them warm, and glanced around the room. Everywhere he looked was gray. It was gray outside the office window and gray inside the office. Would it kill them to paint the walls a different color? The last time he had been at the VA hospital, a woman had come in and given a talk on how colors affect the mood. What idiot would pick gray? He hated going to doctors anyway, but his insurance company required him to have a physical once a year so some new bozo could tell him what he already knew. The doctor he had just seen was at least friendly and had laughed at a few of his jokes, but now he just wished the guy would hurry up. Most of the doctors they sent him to were old and ready to retire or just starting out and in need of guinea pigs to practice on. This one was old. Seventy or more, he guessed. Maybe that's why he was taking so long. Gray walls, gray rug, gray gown, gray doctor.

Finally, the door opened and the doctor came in with his test results. Oswald said, 'So, Doc, will I be able to run in the Boston Marathon again this year?'

This time the doctor ignored Oswald's attempt to be humorous and sat down at his desk, looking rather somber.

'Mr. Campbell,' he said, 'I'm not too happy about what I have to tell you. I usually like to have a family member present at a time like this. I see you have listed your ex-wife as immediate

3

family. Would you like to call and see if she can come in?'

Oswald suddenly stopped wiggling his toes and paid attention. 'No, that's all right. Is there a problem?'

'I'm afraid so,' he said, as he opened his folder. 'I've checked and rechecked your charts and records. I even called in another associate from down the hall, a pulmonary specialist, to consult, but unfortunately he agreed with my diagnosis. Mr. Campbell, I'm going to tell it to you straight. In your present condition you won't live through another Chicago winter. You need to get out of here to a milder climate as soon as possible, because if you don't — well, frankly, I'm not sure I would give you till Christmas.'

'Huh?' Oswald said, as if he were thinking it over. 'Is that right?'

'Yes, it is. I'm sorry to report that since your last checkup the emphysema has progressed to the critical stage. Your lungs were already badly damaged and scarred from the childhood tuberculosis. Add all the years of heavy smoking and chronic bronchitis, and I'm afraid all it would take is one bad cold going into another bout of pneumonia.'

'Is that right? Huh,' Oswald said again. 'That doesn't sound too good.'

The doctor closed his folder and leaned forward on his desk, looked him right in the eye, and said, 'No, it doesn't. In all honesty, Mr. Campbell, considering the alarming rapidity with which this condition has advanced, even with you going to a better climate, the most

4

optimistic prognosis I can give you is a year
. . . maybe two.'

'You're kidding,' said Oswald.

He shook his head. 'No, I'm afraid not. At this
stage, the emphysema is a strain on your heart
and all your other organs. It's not just the lungs
that are affected. Now, I'm not telling you this to
scare you, Mr. Campbell; I only tell you so you
have time to make the appropriate plans. Get
your estate in order.'

As stunned as he was at the news, Oswald
almost laughed out loud at the word *estate*. He
had never had more than two hundred and fifty
dollars in the bank in his entire life.

The doctor continued. 'Believe me, I wish the
diagnosis had been better.' And the doctor meant
it. He hated having to hand out bad news. He
had just met Mr. Campbell, but he had liked the
personable little guy at once. 'Are you sure you
don't need me to call anyone for you?'

'No, that's all right.'

'How will this news affect your future plans,
Mr. Campbell?'

Oswald looked up at him. 'Pretty damn
adversely, I would say, wouldn't you?'

The doctor was sympathetic. 'Well, yes, of
course. I just wondered what your future plans
may have been.'

'I didn't have anything in particular in mind
. . . but I sure as hell hadn't planned on this.'

'No, of course not.'

'I knew I wasn't the picture of health, but I
didn't think I was headed for the last roundup.'

'Well, as I said, you need to get out of Chicago

5

as soon as you can, somewhere with as little pollution as possible.'

Oswald looked puzzled. 'But Chicago is my home. I wouldn't know where else to go.'

'Do you have any friends living somewhere else — Florida? Arizona?'

'No, everybody I know is here.'

'Ah . . . and I assume you are on a limited budget.'

'Yeah, that's right. I just have my disability pension.'

'Uh-huh. I suppose Florida might be too expensive this time of year.'

Never having been there, Oswald said, 'I would imagine.'

The doctor sighed and leaned back in his chair, trying to think of some way to be of help. 'Well, let's see . . . Wait a minute, there was a place my father used to send all his lung patients, and as I remember the rates were pretty reasonable.' He looked at Oswald as if he knew. 'What *was* the name of that place? It was close to Florida . . . ' The doctor suddenly remembered something and stood up. 'You know what? I've still got all his old files in the other room. Let me go and see if by any chance I can find that information for you.'

Oswald stared at the gray wall. Leave Chicago? He might as well leave the planet.

★ ★ ★

It was already dark and still freezing cold when Oswald left the office. As he rounded the corner

6

at the Wrigley Building, the wind from the river hit him right in the face and blew his hat off. He turned and watched it flip over and over until it landed upside down in the gutter and began to float like a boat on down the block. Oh, the hell with it, he thought, until the frigid air blew through what little hair he did have left and his ears started to ache, so he decided to run after it. When he finally caught the hat and put it back on his head he realized he was now wearing wet shoes with no socks, a wet hat, and he had just missed his bus. By the time another bus finally came, he was completely numb from the cold plus the shock of the news he had just received. As he sat down, his eye caught the advertisement above his seat for Marshall Field's department store: MAKE THIS THE BEST CHRISTMAS EVER. START YOUR CHRISTMAS SHOPPING EARLY THIS YEAR. It suddenly dawned on him that, in his case, he had *better* start early and it might already be too late. According to the doctor, if he did live to see it, this Christmas could be his last.

Not that Christmas had ever meant much to him, but still it was a strange thought. As he sat there trying to comprehend the world without him, the bus jerked and lurched in short spurts all the way down State Street, now packed with bumper-to-bumper rush-hour traffic and loud with the angry sounds of the blaring horns of frustrated people. As more passengers began to crowd onto the bus, they weren't in such a good mood either. One woman glared at Oswald and said to her friend, 'Gentlemen used to get up and give a lady a seat.' He thought to himself, *Lady, if I could get up, I would,* but he still couldn't feel his legs.

After about five minutes, when he could begin to move his fingers, he reached in his pocket and pulled out the brochure the doctor had given him. On the front page was a photograph of what looked to be a large hotel, but it was hard to make out. The brochure was faded and looked as if it had water damage, but the print underneath was still legible:

THE WOODBOUND HOTEL
IN
THE SUNNY SOUTH
UNDER NEW MANAGEMENT

Horace P. Dunlap
Formerly of Gibson House, Cincinnati, Ohio

Deep in the southernmost part of Alabama, along the banks of a lazy winding river, lies the sleepy little community known as Lost River, a place that time itself seems to have forgotten.

LOCATION

This pleasant health resort sits nestled between Perdido and Mobile bays, in the subtropical district, especially adapting it for a winter home. To the south lies the Gulf of

Mexico, the soft breezes from which seem at all times to temper the climate. The near presence of a large body of salt water furnishes an atmosphere charged with ozone, chlorine, and other life-giving constituents. Instead of the barren bleakness of the northern winter, there is the luxurious warmth and color of the Southern Clime, where a gloomy day is the exception and where the azure sky and a wealth of sunshine rule. This section of the country, when in the possession of the Spaniards, was called 'The Charmed Belt.'

HEALTH-GIVING CONDITIONS

Many a consumptive, rheumatic, nervous, wornout, and overworked person has found health and a new lease on life by spending a few months in this region; the influence of the saline breezes from the Gulf will bring you a good sharp appetite even if you have not enjoyed a meal for years. *It is the ideal spot for complete recreation and rest from the hustle-bustle whirl of society and the noise of the city. It will quiet your nervous system no matter how badly it may be wrecked. As a winter resort, the climate is all that could be desired and the crystal springwater found everywhere cannot be beat.* 'I would call the entire region one of the garden spots of America,' says Dr. Mark Obecheck of Chicago.

Oswald guessed that must have been his doctor's father. He turned the page and as the bus jerked along he read further.

COMMENTS FROM WINTER VISITORS

Dear Mr. Dunlap,
We so enjoyed the fishing and boating and the pleasant walks in the dense pine woods. The sweet songs of the mockingbird at early morn, the fragrance and balmy air as it drifted into our rooms.
Mr. S. Simms, Chicago, Illinois

Another faded photo captioned: RIVER VIEW FROM THE LARGE VERANDA. He turned the page.

'I fled from the North, from blizzard, frost
and snow
To see the Sunny South where sweet and
balmy breezes blow.'
(A poem by Mrs. Deanne Barkley of Chicago, inspired by a recent winter visit)

Another faded photo: MR. L. J. GRODZIKI AND HIS CATCH OF FINE FISH.

A FISHERMAN'S PARADISE!

Game fish are plentiful here in our southern waters. The following is a partial list of the varieties: redfish, silver and speckled trout, pike, flounder, croakers, mullet, brim, perch, catfish, gar, and tarpon (sometimes

10

called the silver king). Oysters, shrimp, and clams abound.

Another faded photo was captioned A GROUP OF CHICAGO GENTLEMEN ENJOYING A GOOD SMOKE AFTER AN OYSTER BAKE.

Oswald turned the page and there was a photo he could not make out: A ROSEBUSH UNDER WHICH THIRTY PEOPLE CAN STAND COMFORT-ABLY!

As he approached his bus stop he put the booklet back in his pocket and wondered who in the hell would *want* to stand under a rosebush with thirty other people, comfortably or not?

★ ★ ★

When he reached the De Soto Apartment Hotel for Men, where he had lived for the past eight years, a few of the guys were down in the lobby looking at the TV. They waved at him. 'How did it go?'

'Terrible,' he said, blowing his nose. 'I may be dead before Christmas.'

They all laughed, thinking he was joking, and went back to watching the news.

'No, I'm serious,' he said. 'The doctor said I'm in terrible shape.'

He stood there waiting for some reaction, but they weren't paying any attention and he was too tired to argue the point. He went upstairs to his room, took a bath, put on his pajamas, and sat down in his chair. He lit a cigarette and looked out at the blue neon Pabst Blue Ribbon beer

11

sign in the window of his favorite neighborhood bar across the street. Damn, he thought. At a time like this, a man ought to be able to have a drink. But a year ago another doctor had informed him that his liver was shot and if he took one more drink it would kill him. But so what? Now that he was going to die anyway, drinking himself to death might not be such a bad idea after all. It would be fast anyway, and at least he could have a few laughs before he checked out.

He toyed with the idea of getting dressed and heading across the street, but he didn't. He had promised his ex-wife, Helen, he'd stay sober and he would hate to disappoint her again, so he just sat there and tried his best to feel sorry for himself. He had had bad luck from the get-go. He had contracted his first bout of tuberculosis when he was eight, along with 75 percent of the other boys at St. Joseph's Home for Boys, and had been in and out of hospitals fighting chronic bronchitis and pneumonia all his life. Being an orphan, he had never known who he was or where he had come from. Whoever left him on the church steps that night left no clues, nothing except the basket he came in and a can of Campbell's soup. He had no idea what his real name was. Oswald was the next name on St. Joseph's first-name list and, because of the soup, they gave him Campbell as a last name and the initial T. for Tomato, the kind he was found with. Nor did he know his nationality. But one day, when he was about twelve, a priest took a good look at his rather large nose, red hair, and small squinty blue eyes and remarked, 'Campbell, if that's not an Irish mug, I'll eat my hat.' So Oswald guessed he was Irish. Just another piece of bad luck as far as having a problem with booze was concerned.

But it had not been just the drinking. Nothing had come easy to him. School, sports, or girls. He had never been able to keep a job for long, and even the army had released him early with a medical discharge. It seemed to Oswald that everyone else had come into this world with a set of instructions but him. From the beginning he had always felt like a pair of white socks and brown shoes in a roomful of tuxedos. He had never really gotten a break in life, and now it was all over.

After about an hour of trying to work up as much sympathy for himself as he possibly could, he suddenly realized that despite all of his efforts, he wasn't all that upset! At least not as upset as a man *should* be who had just been handed his walking papers. The real truth was, the only two things he would really miss when he checked out were the Cub games and Helen, unfortunately in that order, one of the reasons for their divorce in the first place.

In all honesty, Helen was probably the only one who would really miss him. Although she was remarried with two kids, she was still the person closest to him. He used to go over to her house for dinner quite a bit, but not so much anymore. The new husband was somewhat of a jerk and her two kids had grown from obnoxious young boys into whiny and obnoxious teenagers, who did nothing but give her grief. He couldn't go there anymore without wanting to strangle one or both, so he just didn't go. You can't tell other people how to raise their kids, especially since the other reason for the divorce was because she wanted kids and he didn't. Having spent the first seventeen years of his life in a room with five hundred other screaming and yelling kids, he had had enough of children to last him a lifetime. Still, despite the apparent apathy he felt about his own imminent demise and not knowing the correct protocol for this sort of thing, he supposed he should tell *someone* about his prognosis. He guessed he should tell Helen at least. But after thinking about it a little longer, he wondered why tell her? Given the kind of woman she was, an ex-nurse and a nice person, if she knew how sick he was she would probably insist on his coming to live with them so she could take care of him. Why put her through that? Why worry her? She didn't deserve it. He had caused her enough trouble already. She had enough problems of her own, and besides there *were* those teenagers.

No, he concluded, the best thing he could do for her was just go away and let her get on with her life. Then if he *wanted* to take a drink nobody would be the wiser or care. He just had to find a place he could afford on his small $600-a-month government pension.

He went over and sat down, took the Woodbound Hotel brochure out of his coat

14

pocket, and turned to the next page, where Horace P. Dunlap asked the reader:

WHY GO TO FLORIDA?

Why go to Florida with its low lands and deficiency of good water? Why go to New Mexico and be exposed to alkali dust? Why go to California, with its cold uncomfortable houses two to three thousand miles away, when Baldwin County can be reached from Chicago in twenty-six hours? On both sides of the river you will find a magnificent growth of fine timber. Among the many varieties are the magnolia, sweet bay, sweet gum, Cuban pine, ash, maple, evergreen, and white cedar, with a great variety of shrubs and Spanish moss hanging from the live oaks. Satsuma trees, pecan, kumquat, pear, fig, and apple are plentiful. The winters here are like the northern spring or early autumn. In fact, you can enjoy nature walks in comfort nearly every day of the year . . . Along the river, ducks, geese, wild turkey, dove, quail, raccoon, and squirrel abound. Here is an abundance of sparkling-clear springs, and good water is found at 20 to 30 feet. All the various fruits and vegetables by reason of the mild climate are about two weeks in advance of other sections of the country. What does this mean for the health seeker? It means relief and cure to those who suffer from bronchitis, catarrh, and rheumatism and absolute safety

15

from pneumonia; it means an easy recovery for those few who get grippe in this county. It means a carefree romping out-of-doors for the pale or delicate boy or girl, the joy of picking beautiful flowers at Christmastime.

RENT A LOVELY ROOM OR A DANDY LITTLE BUNGALOW!

We extend a hearty welcome for you to visit our fair county. We are just as large as Chicago, only we haven't quite so many houses. Don't say we are giving you only exaggerations. Come visit and see for yourself the sunshine, flowers, and orange blossoms in December.

On the back page was a song complete with words and music.

'Dreamy Alabama'
Words and music by Horace P. Dunlap

Evening shadows falling
where the southland lies,
whip-poor-will is calling
'neath the starlit skies I love

Dreamy Alabama where sweet folks are waiting,
there my heart is ever turning, all day long.
Dreamy Alabama, where songbirds are singing,
waiting to greet me with their song.

16

Winding river flowing
through the whispering pines
like a stream of silver
when the moonlight shines above.

Oswald put the brochure down. This had to be one of the dullest places in America, but he had to hand it to Horace P. Dunlap. He sure as hell was trying hard to get your business. He had thrown in everything but the kitchen sink. Tomorrow he would give old Horace a call and see how much it would cost to rent a lovely room or a dandy little bungalow, and find out where the nearest bar was.

Hello, Operator

The next morning after his usual thirty to forty-five minutes of coughing, Oswald lit his first cigarette, picked up the phone, and called the number on the brochure.

'I'm sorry, sir, but that number is invalid. Are you sure you have the right number?'

'I know it's the right number. I'm looking at it right now.'

'What area code are you trying to call?'

'Well, I don't know. It's the Woodbound Hotel in Lost River in Baldwin County, Alabama.'

'Let me connect you with information for that area.' In a moment another operator answered. 'May I help you?'

'I hope so. I'm trying to reach the Woodbound Hotel.'

'Just a moment, sir, I'll check that for you right away.' This operator had such a thick southern accent he thought she must be joking with him. 'I'm sorry, sir, but I don't have a listing for a Woodbound Hotel anywhere in Baldwin County.'

'Oh. Well, where are you?'

'I'm in Mobile.'

'Is that in Alabama?'

'Yes, sir.'

'Have you ever heard of a place called Lost River?'

'No, sir, I haven't.'

'Is there a listing for *anything* down there?'

'Just a moment. Let me check that for you . . . Sir, I have a listing for the Lost River community hall and one for the post office. Would you like me to connect you to either one of those numbers?'

'Yes, let me try the first one. They might be able to help me.'

★   ★   ★

Not five minutes earlier, Mrs. Frances Cleverdon, an attractive, slightly plump woman with white hair as soft as spun cotton candy, and her younger sister, Mildred, had just entered the back of the community hall through the kitchen. It was 72 degrees outside and the hall was hot and stuffy, so they opened all the windows and turned on the overhead fans. It was the first Saturday of the month. Tonight was the monthly meeting and potluck dinner of the Lost River Community Association. They were there early to deliver what they had made for the potluck dinner and to get the place ready for the evening. Frances had brought two covered dishes, one a green-bean casserole, the other a macaroni and cheese, and several desserts.

Mildred, who had prepared fried chicken and a pork roast, heard the phone ringing first but ignored it. When Frances came back in from the car, Mildred said, 'Don't answer that. It's

19

probably Miss Alma, and we'll never get her off the phone.'

After another trip to the car for two cakes and three pecan pies, the phone was still ringing.

Frances said, 'You know she's not going to give up,' and picked up the receiver one second before Oswald was going to hang up.

'Hello?'

'Hello!' he said.

'Hello?' she said again.

'Who is this?'

'This is Frances. Who's this?' she asked, in the same southern accent as the operator.

'This is Oswald Campbell, and I'm trying to find the phone number for a hotel.'

'Well, Mr. Campbell, this is the community hall you've reached.'

'I know. The operator gave me this number.'

'The operator? Where are you calling from?'

'Chicago.'

'Oh, my!'

'Do you happen to have the number of the Woodbound Hotel? It's a health resort that's supposed to be down there.'

'The Woodbound Hotel?'

'Have you ever heard of it?'

'Yes, I've heard of it . . . but it's not here anymore.'

'Did it close?'

'Well, no. It burned down.'

'When?'

'Just a minute, let me see if my sister knows.' Frances called out, 'Mildred, when did the old hotel burn down?'

Mildred looked at her funny. 'About 1911, why?'

'Mr. Campbell, it was in 1911.'

'In 1911? You're kidding!'

'No, they say it burned right to the ground in less than an hour.'

'Oh . . . well . . . could you give me the name of another hotel I could call?'

'Down here?'

'Yes.'

'There isn't any.'

'Oh.'

'There used to be a few, but not anymore. If you don't mind me asking, how on earth did you hear about the old Woodbound all the way up there in Chicago?'

'My doctor gave me a brochure, but obviously it was a little out-of-date. Thanks anyway.'

'Hold on a second, Mr. Campbell,' she said, and called out, 'Mildred, close that screen door, you're letting the flies in. I'm sorry, Mr. Campbell. What kind of place were you looking for?'

'Just somewhere to spend a couple of months this winter, get out of the cold weather for a while. I have a little lung problem.'

'Oh, dear. That's not good.'

'No. My doctor said I needed to get out of Chicago as soon as possible.'

'I can understand that. I'll bet it's cold up there.'

'Yes,' he said, trying not to be rude but also wanting to hang up. This call was probably expensive. But Mrs. Cleverdon continued

21

talking. 'Well, it's hot down here. We just had to open the windows and turn all the fans on. Oh. Hold on. Mr. Campbell, I've got to go close that door . . . '

While he was waiting, he could actually hear the sounds of birds chirping in the background over long distance. It must be some of those damn whip-poor-wills, he thought, and they were costing him money.

Frances picked up the phone again. 'Here I am, Mr. Campbell. Now, would this be a place for you and your wife or just you?'

'Just me.'

'Have you tried anywhere else?'

'No. I wanted to try there first, it sounded like a nice place. Oh well, thanks anyway.'

'Mr. Campbell. Wait a minute. Give me your number. Let me see if I can come up with something for you.'

He gave her his number just to get her to hang up. What a crazy place. Evidently they would just talk the head off of any stranger that happened to call.

★   ★   ★

Mildred came back in the kitchen after putting flowers on the two long tables in the other room. 'Who were you on the phone with so long?'

'Some poor man from Chicago with bad lungs who needs a place for the winter. His doctor had given him a brochure for that old hotel, and he thought he might want to come here.' She walked over and pulled out the huge coffeepot.

'Why *did* it burn down, I wonder?'

'They say it was rats and matches.'

'Oh, lord,' said Frances, opening a large dark-brown can of A&P Eight O'Clock coffee. 'They'll just chew on anything, won't they?'

★   ★   ★

Around three o'clock the next afternoon, Oswald was about to pick up the phone and make another call to Florida when it rang. 'Hello?'

'Mr. Campbell, this is Frances Cleverdon, the lady you spoke to in Alabama yesterday. Do you remember me?'

'Yes, of course.'

'Listen, have you found a place yet?'

'No, not yet, not one I can afford, anyway.'

'Yes. Well, if you still have a mind to come down here, I think I found a place for you. We have a very nice lady next door to me, and she said she would be happy to rent you a room for however long you want it.'

'Huh,' said Oswald. 'How much do you think she would charge?'

'She told me that fifty dollars a week would suit her just fine, if that was all right with you. Of course, that would include all your meals. Is that too much?'

Oswald added up his $600-a-month pension, plus the small military medical-discharge check from the government, and figured he could handle it. The places in Florida he called had been double and triple that amount.

23

'No, that rate sounds fine to me. When would it be available?'

'Betty said for you to just come on anytime, the sooner the better; the river is so pretty this time of year. But now, Mr. Campbell, before you decide on anything, I need to warn you. We are just a small place down here, all we have is one grocery store and a post office, but if it's warm weather and peace and quiet you want, I can guarantee you'll get plenty of that.'

'Sounds good to me,' he lied. He couldn't think of anything worse, but the price was right. He figured he should probably grab it before they changed their minds.

'Well, all right then,' she said. 'Just call me back and let me know when you're coming, and we'll have somebody pick you up.'

'OK.'

'But one more thing, Mr. Campbell, just so you know. We are very friendly and sociable down here and good neighbors when you need us, but nobody is going to bother you unless you want them to. By and large we mind our own business.'

★   ★   ★

What Frances had told Mr. Campbell was true. The people in Lost River did mind their own business. However, after having said that, Frances, a romantic at heart, could not help being a little optimistic. With four widows and three single women living in the community, having a new man around would certainly be

24

interesting. One of the three single women was her sister Mildred. Frances was one of the widows, but she did not put herself in the running. She had been very happily married for twenty-seven years and was perfectly content to live on memories, but as for the rest of the ladies she was willing to let fate take a hand. After all, she was a Presbyterian and believed strongly in predestination. Besides, the day Mr. Campbell called happened to be the first Saturday of the month, usually the only day someone was at the hall, and that could not have been just a coincidence. Wouldn't it be wonderful if he turned out to be someone's knight in shining armor? The only other eligible man in Lost River was Roy Grimmitt, who ran the grocery store. But he was only thirty-eight, too young for most of the women. Besides, after what had happened to him, it looked as if Roy was a confirmed bachelor for life. Too bad, she thought, because he was a handsome man and a nice one, but she more than the others understood it. Once you've experienced true love, you don't want anybody else.

The Store

Roy Grimmitt, who ran the grocery store in Lost River, was a big friendly guy and everybody liked him. He was also one of the few people who had actually been born and raised in the area, except for the Creoles across the river, whose families had been there since the 1700s. Roy had inherited the store from his uncle, who had run it for fifty years. The tin Coca-Cola sign across the front of the brick building advertised it simply as GRIMMITT'S GROCERY, but it was much more than that. It was a landmark. If the store had not been on the corner, most people would have driven right by, never knowing there was a river or an entire community of people living there. For the sixty or seventy residents, it was the place where they did their shopping and kept up on all the news, good and bad. It was an especially favorite stopping-off spot for the many fishermen in the area, the place where they bought their tackle and live bait and swapped lies about how many fish they had caught — all except Claude Underwood, the best fisherman there, who never said how many he had caught or where he had caught them. There were two gas pumps outside the store; inside was rather plain, with wooden floors and a meat counter in the back. The only concession to decoration was the large array of mounted fish, game birds, and deer heads that lined the walls and a stuffed red fox on top of the shelf in the back. One of the Creoles, Julian LaPonde, the only taxidermist in the area, had once been a good friend and poker pal of Roy's uncle. Most of the produce was local. Roy bought his meat from area hunters and always had plenty of fresh shrimp, crab, and oysters from the Gulf and fish from the river. He got his milk, poultry, eggs, fruits, and vegetables from nearby farms. Because his was the only store around, he stocked much more than just food and gas; he sold everything from work gloves, rakes, shovels, and pickaxes to rubber boots. Kids loved the store because of its great selection of candy, potato chips, and ice cream, and the deep box of ice-cold drinks he kept by the front door filled with every kind you could want: Orange Crush, root beer, Grapettes, Dr Pepper, and RC Cola. Name it, he had it. But Roy also had something that no other store in the world could offer.

★   ★   ★

It had been just a few weeks after Christmas about five years ago, when Roy heard the popping of guns out in back of the store. A pair of kids that lived back up in the woods had gotten high-powered pump-action BB guns that year and were busy shooting everything in sight. Roy was a hunter and a fisherman, but those damn mean little redneck boys would shoot anything and leave it to die. He hated that, and he walked out the back door and yelled at them, 'Hey, you boys, knock it off!' They immediately scattered back into the woods, but they had just shot something, and whatever it was it was still alive and on the ground flopping around. Roy walked over and picked it up. It was a baby bird.

'Damn those little bastards.' It was a scruffy tiny gray-and-brown thing, so young he could not tell what it was. Probably a sparrow or a mockingbird or a wren of some kind. He had picked up many dead or hurt birds that these boys had shot but this was the youngest by far. It probably had not even learned to fly. He knew he couldn't save it, but he took the little bird back inside the store anyway, wrapped it up in an old sock, and put it in a box in a warm dark place in his office so some hawk or owl or other predator could not get it. At least he could save the baby bird from that and let the thing die in peace. Other than that, there was nothing more he could do for it.

Most of the kids that lived around there were pretty nice and Roy had a good relationship with all of them, but these two new boys were surly. Nobody knew who they were or where they had come from. Somebody said their family lived in an old run-down trailer way back up in the woods. He had never seen the parents, but he had seen the boys throwing rocks at a dog and he had no use for them after that, even less now. Anybody that would deliberately shoot a baby bird ought to have their heads knocked together.

If he could get his hands on them, he would do it himself.

The next morning when he opened the store he had almost forgotten about the baby bird when he heard something chirping away in the sock. He walked over and touched it and up it popped with his mouth wide open, still very much alive and hungry for breakfast.

Surprised, Roy said, 'Well, I'll be damned, you little son of a gun.'

Now he didn't know what to do. This was the first hurt bird he had ever picked up that had survived the night, but this little thing was definitely alive and carrying on like something crazy. He went to the phone and called his veterinarian friend who lived in Lillian, a small town ten miles away.

'Hey, Bob, I've got this baby bird over here, I think it's been shot.'

His friend was not surprised. 'Those kids with the BB guns again?'

'Yeah.'

'What kind of bird?'

'I don't know.' Roy looked over at the bird. 'He's kind of ugly . . . looks like some kind of mud hen. He's gray and brown, I think. Could be some kind of sparrow or mockingbird or — oh, I don't know what the thing is, but it looks like it's hungry. Should I feed it?'

'Sure, if you want to.'

'What should I give it?'

'Give it the same thing its mother would, worms, bugs, a little raw meat.' He laughed. 'After all, Roy, you're its mother now.'

'Oh, great, that's just what I need.'

'And Roy . . . '

'What?'

'Seriously, it probably won't live, but you might want to check and see if you can get those BBs out. If you don't, it will die for sure.'

Roy went over, picked up the bird, and examined it and was surprised at how strong it was as it squawked and struggled to get free. He held out the wings and could see four BBs lodged right under its right wing close to the breast. He got a pair of tweezers. After having to dig around for a moment, he carefully lifted the BBs out one by one as the bird squawked and squirmed in discomfort. 'Sorry, fella, I know that hurts, but I've got to do it, pal.' He cleaned the spot with alcohol and put him back in the sock. Then he went over to the live bait section of the store and pulled out a large English red worm and a few grubs and took a razor blade and chopped up a nice breakfast for the bird, who proceeded to gobble the entire thing down and scream for more.

Roy continued to keep the bird in his office. He did not want anyone to know that he was hand feeding a baby bird three times a day and twice at night. He did not want to take the ribbing he would get from his friends. After all, he was a strapping six-foot-two man, and taking care of a baby bird might have seemed sissylike to them. As the days went by Roy tried not to become too attached. He knew how fragile they were and how hard it was to keep them alive. Every morning he half expected to find it dead, but each morning when he opened the door and heard the bird chirping away, he was secretly as pleased as punch and proud of the little bird for hanging on. He never saw anything want to live so bad in all his life, but he still didn't tell anyone. He planned to keep feeding it, and if it survived he would release it when it got old enough to fly.

Several weeks went by. The bird grew stronger and stronger and pretty soon was hopping all around the room, trying to flap his wings, but he could not seem to get off the ground. Roy noticed that each time he tried he kept falling over to the right. As this continued to happen, Roy began to worry about him. One day he put him in a shoe box and drove him over to his friend Bob's office.

The vet looked the bird over and said, 'That wing is just too badly damaged, Roy. He's never going to be able to fly like he should, and he'll certainly never survive in the wild. We probably should just go ahead and put him to sleep.'

Roy felt as if someone had kicked him in the stomach.

'Do you think so?' he asked, trying to hide his disappointment.

'Yes, I do. You shouldn't keep a wild bird like this inside. It would be cruel, really.'

'Yeah, I guess you're right. I was just hoping he would make it.'

'I can do it for you right now if you want me to.'

'No, it's my bird. I'll do it.'

'All right, that's up to you. I'll give you a

bottle of chloroform. Just put it on some cotton and hold it over the beak; he won't feel anything. He'll just go to sleep.'

Roy put the bird back in the shoe box and drove home, and every time he heard the bird jumping around in the box, trying to get out, he knew his friend was right. It would be cruel to keep a thing meant to be free closed up inside. That night he gave the bird as much food as he would eat, and around nine o'clock he sat down and took out the chloroform and a ball of cotton. He sat there, staring at the bird hopping around the room, jumping on everything in sight and pecking at the papers on his desk. He picked him up and examined him more closely under the light. It was then he noticed that some of his feathers were just beginning to turn from brown to red. Upon closer inspection he began to see the beginnings of a small crest forming on the back of his head and a black mask starting to form around his eyes. Then it hit him. This was a redbird! What a shame, this little guy was not going to get the chance to grow up and become the beautiful bird he was meant to be. Damn! All of a sudden Roy felt like going back in the woods and finding those two boys and cracking their heads together right then and there. Finally, after sitting and staring at the bird for a few more hours, Roy stood up and threw the bottle in the trash can. 'Oh, the hell with it, buddy. See you in the morning.' He turned the lights out and went home to bed. He could no more have put that bird to sleep than fly to the moon.

After that night Roy started keeping the bird

in the front of the store with him. Eventually word got out that a baby redbird was living at the grocery store, and everybody who came in got a big kick out of it. At first the bird sat on the counter beside Roy and hopped all over the cash register, but as the weeks went by he was able to fly in short spurts, many times missing his mark, but he was getting stronger and more active every day, so much so that just in case Roy put a sign on the front door:

DON'T LET THE BIRD OUT!

★   ★   ★

At night when Roy locked up and went home he left the bird in the store so he could have the whole place to himself to roam as freely as he pleased, and roam he did. One morning Roy came in and found he had pecked his way through the top of a Cracker Jack box and was hopping around with a large Cracker Jack stuck on his beak. Roy removed it and laughed. The crazy bird must like Cracker Jacks! From then on he called the bird Jack. But as Roy found out later, Jack also liked Ritz crackers, potato chips, peanut butter, and vanilla wafers, and he especially liked chocolate-covered Buddy Bars. The little bird's appetite for sweets was relentless and not exclusive. He once pecked his way inside a large bag of marshmallows, and by the time Roy found him the next morning he was completely covered with powdered sugar. Eventually, everybody got used to buying things that had been pecked at by Jack first.

Everyone who went in the store got a big kick out of Jack except one person. Frances's younger sister, Mildred, made it clear that she did not like the bird and constantly complained to Frances. 'I just know he walks all over everything,' she said. 'There's little peck holes in everything I pick up. He's just a pest. The last time I was up there he landed in my hair and messed up my hairdo and I had to go home and redo the whole thing.'

Frances, who liked the bird, said, 'Oh, Mildred, he never does that to me. I think he does it just to aggravate you because he knows you don't like him.'

'Well, I don't care what you say, I don't think a place where you sell food is a sanitary place to have a bird, and I told Roy; I said, 'It's a good thing we don't have health inspectors around here, or that bird would be against the law.'

'Then why do you keep going up there if all you are going to do is fuss about that bird night and day?'

'Where else am I going to shop? It's not like we are living in the middle of twenty-five supermarkets. I don't have a choice; I'm stuck. I'm telling you that bird is a nuisance. You can't go up there without having it jump on you. He's a menace to society and that's all there is to it, and I don't want to talk about it anymore.'

Frances said, 'Well, I don't either. Just make out a list of what you want and I'll go and get your groceries for you so I don't have to listen to you complain.'

Mildred looked at her, highly incensed. 'And

just how am I supposed to know what I want until I get there? That's why it's called shopping, Frances!' And with that she marched out the door.

Although Jack was a real handful and, without a doubt, could be a pest at times, he had grown from the tiny ugly mud hen he started out as in life into a beautiful scarlet-red and black-masked bird. With his lipstick-colored beak and shiny little reddish-brown eyes, he looked exactly like a redbird should, but for some reason when Jack looked right at you, he seemed to have a silly smile on his face. One day Roy told Claude Underwood, 'I swear that crazy bird has a sense of humor. Every morning I come in and he's done something else just to make me laugh. I came in yesterday, and the fool was hanging upside down swinging back and forth in the fishnet.'

As time went on, Roy saw how smart the bird was and began to teach him tricks. Pretty soon he had Jack riding around on his finger and eating sunflower seeds out of his hand. His favorite game was when Roy would hide a sunflower seed in someone's pocket and Jack would go inside the pocket of the surprised person and come back out with it and fly over and hand it to Roy. Then Roy would give him ten more.

Jack clearly loved all the attention he was getting. When he saw himself in the mirror for the first time, he hunched down and bobbed his head at his reflection and tried to attack it, so Roy had to get rid of all the mirrors. Jack had made it known that as far as he was concerned the store was his territory, and he did not want another bird around. When the bird in the mirror had disappeared so quickly, Jack was convinced that he and he alone had run the intruder off, so he puffed up and strutted around and became bolder and bolder. Most of the time he rode on Roy's shoulder or on his hat, but he pretty much went where he pleased. Eventually that turned out to be dangerous.

One day, the postmistress Dottie Nivens's big fat orange cat named Henry sat outside the store all day, looking in the window at Jack fluttering around the cash register, just waiting with his tail swishing back and forth, his eyes never losing sight of the bird. He was determined to catch it one way or another. Around three-thirty, when the kids from Lost River got off the school bus from Lillian and started coming in for candy and cold drinks, the cat saw his chance. He lunged through the open screen door, and before anyone saw him he had leaped up on the counter and made a grab for Jack. Jack shot straight up in the air, just barely managing to escape Henry's claws, and landed on top of a shelf. Not to be deterred, Henry went tearing through the store right behind him, knocking racks of potato chips, cigarette cartons, cans and bottles on the floor as he chased Jack all around the room. And then everybody was running through the store chasing the cat and yelling. What a racket! It sounded like an earthquake. Poor Jack with his feathers flying and his crest standing straight up on his head, was hopping and leaping as fast and high

36

as he could, with the cat continuing to miss him by mere inches. Jack somehow flapped and hopped his way all the way to the back of the store and landed on top of the meat counter, and the cat immediately sprang up after him and slid on all four feet all the way down the other end, knocking off bottles of ketchup, barbecue sauce, and horse-radish in his wake. In the meantime, Jack, in one herculean effort, took a tremendous leap from the counter and flapped his wings long enough to land on the deer head, just out of the cat's reach. Roy was finally able to shoo the frustrated Henry out the back door with a broom while Jack, with his feathers still all fluffed up, sat on his safe perch and fussed at the cat as he slunk out of the store.

Jack did not come down for the rest of the day and continued to fuss at Roy for letting the cat inside in the first place. The next day a new sign was added to the screen door:

DON'T LET THE BIRD OUT!
DON'T LET THE CAT IN!

River Route

Back in Chicago, Oswald Campbell met with his insurance agent and signed over his death benefits and anything that might be left from his pension after he died to Helen, stipulating that she spend it on herself and not let those kids get ahold of it. He knew they would anyway, and it galled him, but there was nothing he could do about it. He closed out his bank account and had only a little money left. The train was the cheapest way to go, so he made his reservations. The next morning he phoned Mrs. Cleverdon to tell her when he would arrive and find out the new address to have his pension forwarded.

Frances said, 'Send it in care of Miss Betty Kitchen, River Route Forty-eight.'

'River Route? Is that the name of the street?'

'No, that's the river,' she said.

'Oh. Well, I need a street address.'

'That *is* the address, Mr. Campbell. We get our mail by boat.'

Oswald was confused. 'By boat? I don't have a boat.'

She laughed. 'You don't need a boat, the mailman brings it by boat.'

'Where does he bring it?'

'Right to your dock.'

He was still confused. 'Don't I need a zip code or anything?'

'No, you don't need to fool with that, Mr. Campbell. Our mailman knows where everybody lives.'

'I see . . . so it's just River Route Forty-eight?'

'That's right, I'm River Route Forty-six. My sister Mildred is Fifty-four.' She wanted to mention Mildred to him as much as possible.

Oswald hung up and wondered what kind of place he was headed to. She had not mentioned they got their mail by boat, for God's sake. He was starting to have second thoughts but he had already given up his room and said goodbye to Helen on the phone, so he guessed he'd just go on as planned. After all, he had not told Mrs. Cleverdon he was a walking time bomb and would probably die on them. Besides, it was too late now. He couldn't afford to go anywhere else at this point. He only hoped the grocery store down there sold beer at least. There was no reason to stay sober too long. Not when you had nothing to look forward to anyway.

★ ★ ★

The moment Frances had hung up, she realized that she had forgotten to at least *warn* him about Betty Kitchen's mother, Miss Alma. She thought about calling him back but changed her mind. Maybe it was for the best; after all, she didn't want to scare him off before he even arrived. Besides, she had to run over to Mildred's house and help get ready for the meeting of the Mystic

Order of the Royal Polka Dots Secret Society. Christmas was just around the corner and they had to make arrangements for the Mystery Tree. Every year in the dead of night, all the club members would get together and decorate the large cedar tree standing in front of the community hall. The Polka Dots did a lot of good works and they did all their good works in secret. The club motto was 'To Toot One's Own Horn Is Unattractive.' The only honorary male member of the Polka Dots was Butch Mannich, whom everybody called Stick, because he was six-four and weighed 128 pounds. He was Sybil Underwood's twenty-six-year-old nephew and a good soul who did anything the ladies needed. He supplied the ladder and was the only one tall enough to hang the lights on the top of the tree each year.

★ ★ ★

When Frances walked in the house for the meeting, Mildred was lounging on the couch in the living room wearing a bright floral Hawaiian muumuu and reading the new book she had just borrowed from the bookmobile entitled *Romance on the Bayou: A Steamy Story of Forbidden Love Deep in the Bayou Country of Louisiana*. When Frances saw what her sister was reading, she said, 'Oh, for God's sake, Mildred, when are you going to stop reading all that trash?' Mildred closed the book, laid it on the coffee table, and answered, 'When are you going to stop eating all that candy?'

40

Frances never could get the best of Mildred. As girls they had both attended one of the finest finishing schools in Chattanooga, but even then Mildred had always been somewhat of a maverick. She had been the first girl in town to ever wear a pants suit inside the Chattanooga Country Club: too independent, long before it was fashionable. Frances thought it was probably the reason that the boy Mildred had been engaged to ran off and married someone else. It could also account for the fact that you never knew what color Mildred's hair was going to be the next time you saw her. She dyed her hair on a whim and according to how she felt from day to day. Today it was some sort of plaid. Frances hoped that by the time Mr. Campbell arrived it would be at least close to the color of something natural. But she did not say anything. If Mildred knew she was trying to fix her up with a man she would do something crazy for sure. Frances worried about her sister. Mildred had retired after twenty-five years of work, had good insurance, owned her own home, and had plenty of friends, but she did not seem happy. Frances worried that Mildred was getting bitter as she aged and turning into an old curmudgeon right before her eyes. It was one of the many reasons that Frances was holding such high hopes for Mr. Campbell. Mildred needed to get over that boy who had left her, and move on with her life before it was too late.

Dreamy Alabama

As the doctor had suggested, Oswald tied up all loose ends and settled his estate, a task that took him no more than five minutes. It consisted of throwing away three pairs of old shoes and giving away one of his two overcoats. He packed the one baseball he had caught at a game and all his other belongings into a single suitcase. That night a few of his friends from AA took him out for a farewell cup of coffee. He told them he would most probably be back in the spring. No point in getting anyone upset.

The next morning he took a cab to the L&N railroad station at LaSalle Street. He found his seat, and the train pulled out of the station at 12:45 P.M. As the familiar buildings passed by his window, he knew he was seeing Chicago for the last time and he thought about going to the club car for a drink right then and there, but the 'One Day at a Time' chip his friends had given him last night was still in his pocket. He felt he should probably wait until they got farther away from Chicago and his AA group, so he just sat and looked out the window and soon became preoccupied with the scenery passing by. As they traveled south, through Cincinnati and Louisville to Nashville, the landscape slowly began to change. The deeper south they went, the more the brown land started to turn a different color, and by the time he woke up the next morning the barren black trees that lined the tracks the day before had been replaced with thick evergreens and tall pines. He had gone to sleep in one world and awakened in another. Overnight, the gray gloomy winter sky had turned a bright blue with huge white cumulus clouds so big that Oswald's first thought was, You've got to be kidding!

When they reached Mobile late that afternoon, the moment he stepped off the train, a tall thin man with a small head, who looked to Oswald exactly like a praying mantis wearing a baseball cap, stepped up. 'Are you Mr. Campbell?' He said he was, and the man took his bag and said, 'Welcome to Alabama! I'm Butch Mannich, but you can call me Stick; everybody else does.' As they walked along he added, 'Yeah, I'm so skinny that when I was a child my parents wouldn't let me have a dog because it would keep burying me in the yard.' Then he laughed uproariously at his own joke.

When they came out of the station, the warm air of Mobile was moist and fragrant and a surprise to Oswald. To see it from the train was one thing; to feel it and smell it was another. Their mode of transportation was a truck that Butch apologized for. 'It ain't pretty, but it'll get us there.' Butch was a cheery soul and talked the entire hour and a half it took them to drive down to Lost River. He handed Mr. Campbell his business card, which had a drawing of a big eye in the middle. Underneath was printed:

BUTCH (STICK) MANNICH
PRIVATE INVESTIGATOR
AND PROCESS SERVER

Oswald was surprised. 'Is there a lot of call for private detective work here?'

'No, not yet,' said Butch, a little disappointed. 'But I'm available, ready, willing, and able, just in case.' It was just getting dark as they went over the long Mobile Bay causeway, and they were able to see the last of the sunset. There was nothing but miles of water on both sides and the sun that was now dipping into the bay was so large and orange it almost scared Oswald.

'Is that normal?' he asked Butch.

Butch glanced out the window. 'Yeah, we get a nice sunset most of the time.'

By the time they turned off the highway to Lost River it was pitch-black outside. 'There's the store,' said Butch, as they whizzed by. Oswald looked out but saw nothing. They drove about a block and stopped in front of a large house. 'Here we are, safe and sound.'

Oswald took out his wallet. 'What do I owe you?'

Butch's reaction was one of genuine surprise. 'Why, you don't owe me a thing, Mr. Campbell.'

★ ★ ★

Just as Oswald reached out to knock on the door, it was flung open by a huge woman,

44

standing at least six feet tall. 'Come on in!' she said, in a booming voice, and snatched his suitcase away from him before he could stop her. 'I'm Betty Kitchen, glad to have you.' She grabbed his hand, shook it, and almost broke it. 'Breakfast is at seven, lunch at twelve, and dinner at six. And if you see a little funny-looking woman spooking around don't let it bother you; it's only Mother. She doesn't know where she is half the time, so if she wanders in your room just chase her out. Let me show you around.'

The house had a long hallway down the middle, and he trailed behind her. She walked to the back of the house, pointing as she went: 'Living room, dining room, and this is the kitchen.' She switched the lights on and then off. She turned around, headed back to the front, and pointed to a small door under the stairs. 'And this is where I sleep,' she said. She opened the door, and inside was a closet just big enough for a single bed. 'I like to be close to the kitchen where I can keep an eye on Mother. It's small but I like it; it reminds me of being on a train. I always slept well on a train, and I was on a lot of them in my day. Come on upstairs. I'll show you your room.'

As he followed her up the stairs, Oswald felt that there was something familiar about her manner and her way of speaking. It was almost as if he had met her before, but he was sure he had not; she was a person you would not forget.

'Mother used to be a baker in Milwaukee, specialized in petits fours and fancy cakes, but that was before she slipped on a cigar wrapper.'

She turned around and looked at him. 'You don't smoke cigars, do you?'

Oswald quickly said no. Even if he had, from the tone of her voice he would have quit on the spot. 'No, I have emphysema; that's why I'm here. For my health.'

She sighed. 'Yes, we get a lot of that. Most of the people that come down here have something or another the matter with them . . . but not me. I'm as healthy as a horse.' That was evident as they walked into his room and she heaved his suitcase onto the bed with one arm. 'Well, here it is, the sunniest room in the house. It used to be mine before I moved downstairs. I hope you like it.'

He looked around and saw it was a spacious open room with yellow floral wallpaper and a small yellow sofa in the corner. The brown spindle bed was made up with a crisp white chenille spread, and above it hung a framed embroidered plaque that read HOME SWEET HOME.

She pointed at two doors. 'Closet to the left, bathroom on the right, and if you need anything just holler. If not, see you at oh-seven-hundred.'

He went in the bathroom and was surprised to see it was almost as big as the bedroom, with a green sink and tub. Another surprise: It had a window. He had never seen a bathroom with a window. He was so tired he just wanted to go lie down, but he felt grimy from the train ride so he took a bath and put his pajamas on and got into the soft bed with its clean sweet-smelling sheets. He lay there and looked around his new room once more before he turned off his lamp and fell into a deep peaceful sleep.

★   ★   ★

After Oswald had gone upstairs to bed, the phone rang. It was Frances calling Betty to inquire if Mr. Campbell had arrived safe and sound. After she was told yes, Frances's next question was, 'Well?'

Betty laughed. 'Well . . . he's a cute little man, with crinkly blue eyes and red hair. He sort of looks like an elf.'

Frances said, 'An elf?'

'Yes, but a nice elf.'

Somewhat disappointed that Mr. Campbell was not as handsome as she had hoped for — Mildred was so picky where men were concerned — nonetheless Frances looked on the bright side. An elf, she thought. Oh, well, it *is* close to Christmas. Maybe it was some kind of sign. After all, hope springs eternal.

★   ★   ★

Oswald opened his eyes at six-thirty the next morning to a room filled with sunlight and with the sound of those same birds chirping he had heard over the phone, only twice as loud. To a man used to waking up for the past eight years in a dark hotel room around nine-thirty or ten to the sounds of traffic, this was unsettling. He tried to go back to sleep but the birds were relentless and he started coughing, so he got up. As he was

47

dressing, he noticed an advertisement on the wall that Betty Kitchen had obviously cut out of a magazine. It was a picture of a ladies' dressing table and alongside a compact, lipstick, comb, and a pack of Lucky Strike Green cigarettes was a WAC dress uniform hat. The caption underneath said SHE MAY BE A WAC — BUT SHE'S A WOMAN TOO!

Then it dawned on him. That's what had seemed so familiar. The old gal must have been in the service, probably as an army nurse. God knows he had been around enough army nurses, in and out of so many VA hospitals. He had even married one, for God's sake. Downstairs in the kitchen, while eating a breakfast of eggs, biscuits, grits, and ham, he found out he was right. Not only had she been an army nurse, she was a retired lieutenant colonel, supervisor of nurses, and had run several big hospitals in the Philippines.

He informed her that he had been in the army as well.

She looked up. 'Somehow, Mr. Campbell, I wouldn't have pegged you for a military man.'

He laughed. 'Neither did they. I never got out of Illinois.'

'Ah, that's too bad.'

'Yeah, I guess, but I don't have any complaints. I got a nice medical discharge and went to school, thanks to the old US of A Army.'

About that time, the mother, who was half as tall as her daughter and looked like a dried-up little apple doll, appeared in the doorway. She ignored Oswald and seemed highly agitated.

48

'Betty, the elephants are out in the yard again. Go see what they want.'

'Yes, Mother,' said Betty. 'I'll go find out in just a minute. Go on back upstairs now.'

'Well, hurry up. They're stepping all over my camellia bushes.'

After she left, Betty turned to him. 'See what I mean? She thinks she sees all kinds of things out in the yard. Last week it was flying turtles.' She walked over and picked up his dishes. 'I'm not sure if it was that fall she took a while ago or just her age; she's older than God.' She sighed. 'But that's the Kitchen curse, longevity — on both sides. How about yourself, Mr. Campbell? Do you have longevity in your family?'

Not having any information about his real family, but considering his own current condition, he said, 'I sincerely doubt it.'

★ ★ ★

After breakfast, Oswald went back to his room and finished unpacking, and a few minutes later he heard Betty call up the stairs, 'Yoo-hoo! Mr. Campbell! You have a visitor!'

When he came out, a pretty woman in a white blouse and a blue skirt looked up and said, 'Good morning!' He recognized the voice at once and went downstairs to meet Frances Cleverdon. Although her hair was white, he was surprised to see that up close she had a youthful-looking face, with blue eyes and a lovely smile. She handed him a large welcome basket filled with pecans, a cranberry cream-cheese

49

coffee cake, little satsuma oranges, and several jars of something. 'I hope you like jelly,' she said. 'I made you some green pepper and scuppernong jelly.'

'I do,' he said, wondering what in hell a scuppernong was.

'Well, I won't stay, I know you must be busy. I just wanted to run in for a second and say hello, but as soon as you get settled in and feel like it, I want you to come over for dinner.'

'Well, thank you, Mrs. Cleverdon, I will,' he said.

As she got to the door, she turned and asked if he had been down to the store and met Roy yet.

'Not yet,' he said.

'No?' She smiled as if she knew a secret. 'You need to go and see what's down there. I think you're in for a treat.'

After she left, Oswald guessed he should take a walk and at least see the place, and he asked Betty how to find the store. She instructed him to go out the front door, take a left, and it was four houses past the post office at the end of the street.

When he opened the door and walked out onto the porch, the temperature was the same outside as it was inside. He still could not believe how warm it was. Just two days ago he was in an overcoat and icy rain, and today the sun was shining and he was in a short-sleeve shirt. He went out, took a left, and saw what he had not been able to see last night.

The street was lined on both sides by fat oak trees, with long gray Spanish moss hanging from each one. The limbs of the oaks were so large that they met in the middle and formed a canopy of shade in each direction for as far as he could see. The houses he passed on both sides of the street were neat little well-kept bungalows, and in every yard the bushes were full of large red flowers that looked like roses. As he walked along toward the store, the fattest squirrels he had ever seen ran up and down the trees. He could hear birds chirping and rustling around in the bushes, but the undergrowth of shrubs and palms was so thick he couldn't see them. He soon passed a white house with two front doors and an orange cat sitting on the steps. One side of the house had POST OFFICE written above the door.

As he went by, the door opened and a thin willowy woman with stick-straight bangs came out and waved at him. 'Hello, Mr. Campbell. Glad you're here!'

He waved back, although he had no idea who she was or how she knew his name. When he got to the end of the street he saw a redbrick grocery store building with two gas pumps in front and went in. A clean-cut man with brown hair, wearing khaki pants and a plaid shirt, was at the cash register.

'Are you Roy?' Oswald asked.

'Yes, sir,' the man said, 'and you must be Mr. Campbell. How do you do.' He reached over and shook his hand.

'How did you know who I was?'

Roy chuckled. 'From the ladies, Mr. Campbell. They've all been waiting on you. You don't know how happy I am you are here.'

'Really?'

'Oh, yeah, now they have another single man to pester to get married besides me.'

Oswald put his hands up. 'Oh, Lord, they don't want me.'

'Don't kid yourself, Mr. Campbell. If you're still breathing they want you.'

'Well' — Oswald laughed — 'I'm still breathing, at least for the moment.'

'Now that you're here we have to stick together and not let any of those gals catch us off guard. Unless, of course, you're in the market for a wife.'

'Noooo, not me,' said Oswald. 'I've already made one poor woman miserable. That's enough.'

Roy liked this little guy right away. 'Come on back to the office and let me get you a cup of coffee, and I'll introduce you to my partner.'

As they walked back, Roy whistled and called out, 'Hey, Jack!'

Jack, who had been busy all morning running up and down the round plastic bird wheel with bells that Roy had ordered through the mail, heard the whistle, flew out of the office, and landed on Roy's finger.

Oswald stopped dead in his tracks. 'Whoa. What's that?'

'This is Jack, my partner,' Roy said, looking at the bird. 'He really owns the place. I just run it for him.'

'My God,' said Oswald, still amazed at what he saw. 'That's a cardinal, isn't it?'

Roy held Jack away from him so he could not hear and confided, 'Yes, officially he's a cardinal, but we don't tell him that; we just tell him he's just a plain old redbird. He's too big for his britches as it is.' Then he spoke to the bird. 'Hey, Jack, tell the man where you live.'

The bird cocked his head and Oswald swore the bird chirped with the same southern accent Roy had. It sounded exactly like he was saying, 'Rite cheer! . . . Rite cheer! . . . Rite cheer!'

When Roy was busy waiting on some customers, Oswald wandered around the store, examining the mounted fish and stuffed animals that covered the walls. They looked almost alive. The red fox seemed so real Oswald jumped when he first saw him up on the counter. He later remarked to Roy, 'That's really nice stuff you have here. For a second I thought that damn fox was alive. And those fish up there are really great.'

Roy glanced up at them. 'Yeah, I guess so. My uncle put them up there. He won most of them in a poker game.'

'Who did them, somebody local?'

'Yeah, Julian LaPonde, an old Creole, lives across the river.'

'A Creole? What's that? Are they Indians?'

Roy shook his head. 'Who knows what they are — they claim to be French, Spanish, Indian, you name it.' He indicated the mounted animals. 'And in that guy's case, I'm sure there's a little weasel thrown in.' He changed the subject. 'All those fish you see up there were caught by our mailman, Claude Underwood. That speckled trout is a record holder. Do you fish? 'Cause if you do, he's the man to see.'

'No,' Oswald admitted, 'I'm not much of a fisherman, or a hunter either, I'm afraid.' He wouldn't have known a speckled trout from a mullet.

★ ★ ★

Oswald had spent about an hour roaming around the store and watching that crazy redbird of Roy's run around on his wheel when the phone rang. Roy put the phone down and called out, 'Hey, Mr. Campbell, that was Betty. She said your lunch is ready.'

Oswald looked at his watch. It was exactly twelve o'clock, on the dot. 'Well, I guess I'd better go.'

'Yep, you don't want to get her riled. Hey, by the way, have you met the mother?'

'Oh, yes,' Oswald said, rolling his eyes.

'They say she's harmless, but I'd lock my door at night if I were you.'

'Really? Do you think she's dangerous?'

'Well,' said Roy, looking up at the ceiling, 'far be it from me to spread rumors, but we don't know what happened to the daddy, now, do we?' By the look on Oswald's face, Roy could tell he was going to have a lot of fun kidding around with him. He would believe anything he told him.

As he left the store and headed back, Oswald realized he had been so busy looking at Jack and talking he forgot to notice if the store sold beer.

Oh, well, there was always tomorrow.

When he got home he asked Betty about the woman with the bangs at the post office who had waved at him, twice now. 'Oh, that's Dottie Nivens, our postmistress. We got her from an ad we put in *The New York Times*. We were afraid when she got here that she'd see how small we were and leave, but she stayed and we sure are glad. She gives one wingding of a party and makes a mean highball; not only that, she can jitterbug like nobody's business.' Oswald wondered if the postmistress might be a little off her rocker as well, to leave New York City for this place.

★ ★ ★

Around twelve-thirty, while Oswald was having his lunch, Mildred, who had been in Mobile all morning buying Christmas decorations for the Mystery Tree with money from the Polka Dots' jingle-bell fund, called Frances the minute she got home and said, 'Well?'

Frances, trying to be tactful, said, 'Well . . . he's a cute little man, with cute little teeth, and of course he has that funny accent and . . . '

'And what?'

Frances laughed in spite of herself. 'He looks like an elf.'

'Good Lord.'

'But a nice elf,' she quickly added. Mildred was always one to make snap judgments, and Frances did not want her to make up her mind about Oswald before she even met him. She could be so cantankerous.

★ ★ ★

As a rule, Oswald rarely ate three whole meals in one day, but on his first day, in Lost River, after a huge breakfast, for lunch he ate baked chicken, a bowl of big fat lima beans, mashed potatoes, three pieces of corn bread and honey with real butter (not the whipped margarine spread he usually bought), and two pieces of homemade red velvet cake. He had not had real home cooking since he had been married to Helen and since the divorce he had been eating out at greasy spoons or off a hot plate in his room. That night at dinner he finished everything on his plate, plus two servings of banana pudding, which pleased Betty no end. She liked a man with a big appetite.

He was still somewhat tired and weak from the trip and went up to bed right after dinner. As he reached the top of the stairs, the mother, who had no teeth, poked her head out of her room and yelled, 'Have the troops been fed yet?'

He did not know what to say so he said, 'I think so.'

'Fine,' she said, and slammed her door.

Oh dear, thought Oswald. And even though he suspected that Roy had been kidding around with him earlier, he did lock his door that night, just in case.

★ ★ ★

The next morning the birds woke him up once more, but he felt rested and hungry again. While eating another big breakfast, he asked what had brought Betty and her mother all the way from Milwaukee to Lost River, Alabama.

Betty threw four more pieces of bacon into the pan. 'Well, my friend Elizabeth Shivers, who at the time worked for the Red Cross, was sent here to help out after the big hurricane, and when she got here she just fell in love with the area and moved down, and when I came to visit her, I liked it too so I moved here myself.' She flipped the bacon over and mused. 'You know, it's a funny thing, Mr. Campbell, once people find this place, they don't seem to ever want to leave.'

'Really? How long have you lived here?'

Betty said, 'About fourteen years now. We moved down right after Daddy died.'

At the mention of the father, Oswald tried to sound as casual as possible. 'Ah . . . I see. And what did your father die of, if I may ask?'

'Will you eat some more eggs if I fix them?' she asked.

'Sure,' he said.

She went over to the icebox and removed two more eggs, cracked them and put them in the frying pan, and then said, 'Well, to answer your question, we're really not sure what Daddy died of. He was twenty-two years older than Mother at the time, which would have put him right at a hundred and three. I suppose it could have been old age, but with the Kitchens you never know. All I know is that it was a shock to us all when it happened.'

Oswald felt better. Obviously the old man's exit from the world had not been by violent means as Roy had suggested, but at age 103, just how much of a shock could it have been?

★ ★ ★

The following morning when he went downstairs, Betty Kitchen looked at him and said, 'That's quite a cough you have there, Mr. Campbell. Are you sure you're all right?'

Oswald quickly downplayed it. 'Oh, yeah . . . I think I may have caught a little cold coming down, but I feel fine.' He realized he would have to cough quieter and try not to let her hear him from now on.

After breakfast he thought he would take another walk and asked Betty where the river was. 'Right out the kitchen door,' she said.

Oswald walked out the back of the house into a long yard filled with the tallest pine, evergreen, and cedar trees he had ever seen. He figured some must have been at least six or eight stories high. As he walked toward the river, the fresh early morning air reminded him of the smell of the places around Chicago where they sold Christmas trees each year.

He followed a small path that had been cut through the thick underbrush, filled with pine needles and pinecones the size of pineapples, until he came to a wooden dock and the river. He was amazed at what he saw. The bottom of the river was sandy and the water was as clear as gin — and he should know. He walked out onto the dock, looked down, and could see small silver fish and a few larger ones swimming around in the river. Unlike Lake Michigan, this water was as calm as glass.

As he stood there looking, huge pelicans flapped down the river not more than four feet away from him, flying not more than two inches off the water. What a sight! He had seen pictures of them in magazines and had always thought they were all gray. He was surprised to see that in person they were many colors, pink and blue and orange, with yellow eyes and fuzzy white feathers on their heads. A few minutes later they flew off and then came back and crashed with a loud splash and floated around with their long beaks in the water. He had to laugh. If they had been wearing glasses they would have looked just like people. The only other birds he had ever seen this close up were a few pigeons that had landed on his windowsill at the hotel.

The river was not very wide, and he could see the wooden docks of the houses on the other side. Each one had a mailbox, including the one he was on; he looked down and saw the number 48 on it, as Frances had said. So far, everything he had been told or had read about Lost River in that old hotel brochure was true. Old Horace P. Dunlap had not been lying after all. Who would have guessed Oswald would now be living in one of those dandy little bungalows that old Horace had talked about. From that day just a month ago, when he was headed for the doctor's office, to today, his life had taken a 180-degree turn. Everything was upside down. Even the seasons were flipped. In his wildest dreams, Oswald could never have imagined a month ago that he would wind up in this strange place, with all these strange people. As far as he was concerned, he might just as well have been shot out of a cannon and landed on another planet.

★   ★   ★

The next day he did not know what to do with himself, so after breakfast he asked Betty what time the mail came. She said anywhere between ten and eleven, so he went down to the dock and waited. At about ten-forty-five a small boat with a motor came around the bend. As Oswald watched, the man in the boat went from mailbox to mailbox, opening the lid and skillfully throwing the mail in while the boat slid by. He was a stocky man in a jacket and a cap who looked to be about sixty-five or seventy years of age. When he saw Oswald, he pulled up and turned off his motor.

'Hello, there. You must be Mr. Campbell. I'm Claude Underwood. How are you?'

'I'm fine, happy to meet you,' said Oswald.

Claude handed him a bundle of mail wrapped in a rubber band. 'How long have you been here?'

'Just a few days.'

'Well, I'm sure the ladies are glad you're here.'

'Yeah, it seems they are,' Oswald said. 'Uh, say, Mr. Underwood, I'm curious about this river. How big is it?'

'About five or six miles long. This is the

narrow part you're on now. The wide part is back that way.'

'How do you get to it?'

'Do you want to take a ride with me sometime? I'd be happy to show it to you.'

'Really? I sure would. When?'

'We can go tomorrow, if you like. Just meet me at the post office around nine-thirty and bring a jacket. It gets cold out there.'

Walking back home, Oswald thought it was pretty funny that Mr. Underwood would worry about him getting cold anywhere down here. It might say December on the calendar, but the weather felt just like a Chicago spring and the beginning of baseball season to him.

★　★　★

The next morning, as Oswald walked up to the porch of the post office, a striking-looking woman wearing a lime-green pants suit came out of the other side of the house. The minute she saw Oswald she almost laughed out loud. Frances had described him perfectly. She walked over and said, 'I know who you are. I'm Mildred, Frances's sister, so be prepared. She's already planning a dinner party, so you might as well give up and come on and get it over with.' Mildred chuckled to herself all the way down the stairs. Oswald thought she was certainly an attractive, saucy woman, very different from her sister. She had a pretty face like Frances, but he had never seen hair that color in his life.

He went inside the post office and met Dottie

Nivens, the woman who had waved to him the first morning. She shook his hand and did an odd little half curtsy and said in a deep voice, 'Welcome, stranger, to our fair community.' She could not have been friendlier. Oswald noted that if she had not had a large space between her two front teeth and such straight hair she could be a dead ringer for one of Helen's sisters.

He walked through the door and found Claude in the back of the post office, sorting the last of the mail and putting it in bundles. As soon as Claude finished he put it on a small cart with wheels and they walked to his truck and drove a few blocks down a dirt road to an old wooden boathouse. 'This is where I keep my boat,' he said. 'I used to keep it behind the store, but those redneck boys that moved here shot it up so bad I had to bring it up here.' When they got in the boat Oswald looked around for a life jacket but did not see one. When he asked Claude where it was, Claude looked at him like he thought he was kidding. 'A life jacket?'

'Yes. I hate to admit it, but I can't swim.'

Claude dismissed his concern. 'You don't need a life jacket. Hell, if you do fall in, the alligators will eat you before you drown.' With that, he started the motor and they were off, headed up the river. Oswald hoped he was kidding but was careful not to put his hands in the water just in case he wasn't. As they rounded the bend and went under the bridge and on out the length and breadth of the river was amazing. It was extremely wide in the middle, with houses up and down on both sides. As they went farther north, delivering the mail at every dock, Claude maneuvered the boat inside tiny inlets where the water in some spots could not have been more than six or seven inches deep, opening mailboxes of all sizes, tall and low, and while the boat was moving past them, he never missed a beat or a mailbox.

Oswald was impressed. 'Have you ever missed?'

'Not yet,' Claude said, as he threw another bundle of mail in a mailbox. 'But I'm sure the day will come.'

On some of the docks people were waiting and said hello, and on some dogs ran out barking and Claude reached in his pocket and threw them a Milk-Bone.

'Have you ever been bitten?'

'Not yet.'

About an hour later, they turned around and headed back the way they came. Oswald noticed that Claude did not deliver mail on the other side of the river. When he asked him about it, Claude said, 'No, I don't go over to that side anymore. I used to but that's where the Creoles live. They have their own mailman now.'

Oswald looked across and asked, 'Is that where that Julian LaPonde lives?'

'How do you know about Julian LaPonde?' Claude said.

'Roy told me he mounted all those fish and animals at the store.'

'Huh,' said Claude, lighting his pipe. 'I'm surprised he even mentioned him.' But he did not say why he was surprised.

'Well, he sure is a good taxidermist, but I got the impression that Roy doesn't think much of him as a person.'

'No, he doesn't,' said Claude, and left it at that.

They had been out on the river about two and a half hours when they returned to the boathouse. Oswald was exhausted and as he got out of the boat his legs were shaky. He needed a nap. All that fresh air was too much for one day. He asked Claude what he did after he got off from work every day.

Claude's eyes lit up. 'Ah. Then I go fishing.'

Dinner at Eight

Oswald had been unable to avoid running into Frances Cleverdon, since she lived right next door, and finally agreed to have dinner at her house the next week. After all, he could not hurt her feelings; she had been responsible for his coming to Lost River in the first place.

Frances's house was a neat blue bungalow. It was very nice inside as well, with a completely pink kitchen — pink stove, icebox, and sink — right down to the pink-and-white tiles on the floor. Frances showed him her prize gravy boat collection, and Mildred, whose hair to Frances's dismay was now the color of root beer, remarked, 'I'll never understand why anybody in their right mind would collect gravy boats.' Although Oswald had not wanted to go that night, the food was delicious, especially the macaroni and cheese, and after dinner they played a good game of gin rummy.

However, much to her sister's disappointment, Mildred did *nothing* to help things along in the romance department. All she did all night was crab and complain about everything under the sun, including how much she hated that bird Roy had up at the store, and in between her complaints about Jack she managed to tell several blue jokes that Oswald laughed at. Frances smiled, but was secretly horrified and wanted to strangle her sister. How was she ever going to get a man? A perfectly good dinner wasted, as far as she was concerned.

The next day, true to form, Mildred was back down at the store fussing at Jack, who fluttered around her head. She said, 'You've heard about the four-and-twenty blackbirds baked in a pie? Well, mister, I'm going to bake one big redbird pie if you don't quit pestering me!'

Roy laughed. 'You better watch out, boy, or she'll have you for dinner one day.'

Despite all her complaints Roy liked Mildred a lot. He got a kick out of her and how she was always dyeing her hair different colors. Besides, as Oswald had just found out, she sure could tell a joke.

★ ★ ★

After just a few weeks, Oswald found that he was beginning to get into a routine. Every morning after breakfast he would go to the store, hang around awhile, and then go down to the dock to smoke cigarettes and wait for Claude Underwood to come by with the mail. He didn't dare smoke in Betty's house. As he sat waiting, sometimes for an hour or two, he saw that the river was full of things he had never seen before. All kinds of large birds, loons and egrets, geese and ducks of different kinds, swam up and down the river. A few swam in pairs but most were in flocks that took off together and landed in the water together.

One day while he was waiting, Oswald noticed a black duck out in the river all by himself and he wondered about it. Why did this one lone duck not swim with a mate or with the flock? Did the duck even know he was supposed to be with the others? What had caused that duck to separate from the rest? The more he watched it out there, swimming around, the sadder it made him. He realized he was just like that duck. All his life he had been out in the world alone while the rest of the world swam by, happy in their own flock, knowing who they were and where they belonged.

Oswald was feeling a little sad these days anyway. Christmas was just around the corner, and Betty was already playing Christmas carols on the radio. He supposed it put some people in a good mood, but all those 'I'll be home for Christmas' and 'There's no place like home for the holidays' songs just made him feel lousy. For him, Christmas had always been a season with everything set up just to break your heart. As a kid, all he had ever gotten were cheap toys handed out by a bunch of once-a-year do-gooders, toys that by the next day were either broken or stolen. Even as an adult, when he had spent the holidays with Helen's family, it just made him feel more of an outsider than ever. Each year was the same; all her brothers and sisters would sit around, looking at home movies and reminiscing about their wonderful childhood Christmases. No, Christmas for him had always been like someone shining a great big spotlight down in that dark empty space inside him, and the only way he had been able to handle it in the past was to get drunk. A hangover was nothing compared to feeling all alone in a roomful of people. This year he would be spending what could turn out to be his very last Christmas on the river with the birds and ducks. That, he guessed, was better than nothing.

★ ★ ★

The next time Oswald went in the store he found himself eyeing the cartons of beer stacked over in the corner and was almost headed over there but when Betty Kitchen came in, he decided to stick to his original plan and asked Roy if there was some kind of book he could get so he could try and figure out what kinds of birds and ducks he was looking at. Roy said, 'Come on back in the office with me, I think I have something for you.' The office was a mess, with stacks of papers and old ledgers and Jack's toys everywhere, but Roy rummaged through a pile on the floor and handed Oswald an old ripped paperback copy of *Birds of Alabama: A Birdwatcher's Guide*.

'May I borrow this?' asked Oswald.

'Oh hell, you can have it. I don't need it.'

Oswald took the book up to his room. While he was thumbing through it, he found an old postcard from 1932 that described Lost River as

A magical spot, invisible from the highway by reason of its location in masses of shade

68

trees, along the winding banks of the river, where it lies in a setting of flowers and foliage and songbirds, like a dream of beauty ready for the brush and canvas of the landscape painter.

That's the damn truth, he thought. It *would* be a great place for a painter or a birdwatcher. Then it dawned on him that he, Oswald T. Campbell, was actually studying to become a birdwatcher. Birdwatching was certainly not one of the things he would ever have put on his THINGS TO DO list. As a matter of fact, he had never even had a THINGS TO DO list, and now it was almost too late to do anything. Oh, well, he thought, live and learn. Better late than never. And then he wondered why in the hell he was thinking in clichés.

From that day on, after he had gone down and had a cup of coffee with Roy and shot the breeze with him for a while, he would take his birdwatcher's guide and go down to the river and try to match the birds he was seeing with the pictures in the book. So far he had identified a great blue heron that cracked him up by the way it walked. It picked its feet up and down as if it were stepping in molasses. He had seen cranes, a snowy egret, mallards, wood ducks, and a belted kingfisher, and by December 19 he had already identified his first pileated woodpecker. He was hoping to see an osprey one of these days.

★ ★ ★

On the morning of December 22, when Oswald walked over to the store for coffee with Roy, he saw that the huge cedar tree outside the community hall had been decorated with hundreds of Christmas ornaments and silver and gold tinsel. When he went in the store, he asked Roy who had done it. Roy shook his head.

'We don't know. Every Christmas it happens overnight and nobody knows who did it, but I have my theories. I think it's that bunch of crazy women that do it.'

'Who?'

'Oh, Frances, Mildred, and Dottie; probably Betty Kitchen is in on it, too. I can't prove it but I'll tell you this: Anytime you see all of them wearing polka dots on the same day, watch out.'

Just then the door opened and Frances Cleverdon walked in, looking sunny and cheerful. 'Well, good morning, Mr. Campbell,' she said with a smile. 'How are you getting along?'

'Oh, fine,' he said.

'I hope you're coming to the annual Christmas Eve Dinner at the community hall. Roy's coming, aren't you? We're going to have a lot of good food.'

Roy said, 'I'll be there. Hey, Frances, have you seen the tree yet?' He winked at Oswald as she turned around and looked across the street.

'Well, for heaven's sake!' she said, feigning surprise. 'When did that happen?'

'Last night.'

Frances turned to Oswald. 'Last year the same exact thing happened on the twenty-third. I just wish I knew who was doing it.'

'Yeah, me too,' said Roy. 'I was just telling Mr. Campbell, it's a mystery, all right.'

Walking back home Frances was so pleased. The Polka Dots had done it again! Frances and Betty Kitchen had started the club twelve years ago and the founding members, after herself and Betty, were Sybil Underwood and, later, Dottie Nivens and Mildred. They had named themselves after a Mardi Gras group over in Mobile because they wanted to have fun as well as do good works. And thanks to Dottie Nivens and her amazing ability to make delicious highballs, which they drank out of polka-dotted martini glasses after every meeting, they did have fun. When their friend Elizabeth Shivers over in Lillian heard about it she started another secret society, the Mystic Order of the Royal Dotted Swiss. They also did a lot of good work, but Frances was convinced that they could never top the Mystery Tree caper.

The Christmas Dinner

Oswald had always been shy and was no good at social events. Although it was the last thing on earth he wanted to do, it seemed that on Christmas Eve he had no choice but to put on his one blue suit and tie and go with Betty and her mother to the Dinner and Tree Lighting Ceremony at the community hall. It was made clear to him over and over that everyone was expecting him. So at five-thirty he and Betty Kitchen and her mother, Miss Alma, wearing three giant red camellias in her hair, strolled down the street. It was still about 69 degrees outside and hard for Oswald to believe it was really December twenty-fourth. When they arrived, the hall was already packed with people, and the minute they saw Oswald everyone made a point to come up and shake his hand and welcome him to the area. After about thirty minutes of being pulled around the room like a wooden toy, Oswald was thrilled to see Roy Grimmitt come in, looking as uncomfortable in his blue suit and tie as Oswald felt in his. At around six-thirty, after a prayer was said, it was time to eat and someone called out, 'Let Mr. Campbell start the line.'

Oswald was handed a plate and pushed to the

long table, full of more food than he had ever seen: fried chicken, ham, turkey, roast beef, pork chops, chicken and dumplings, and every kind of vegetables, pies, and cakes you can imagine. At the end sat two huge round cut-glass punch bowls of thick, delicious-smelling eggnog. One was labeled LEADED, the other bowl said UNLEADED. Oswald hesitated for a moment and seriously thought about it, but at the last second went for the unleaded. He did not want to get drunk and make a fool out of himself and embarrass Frances. After all, everyone knew she was responsible for getting him there. The long tables with the white tablecloths had center-pieces decorated with sprigs of fresh holly and pinecones that had been dipped in either shellac or gold or silver paint and sprinkled with glitter. On the pine walls, huge red paper bells hung from twisted red and green crepe paper that wrapped around the room, interspersed with pictures of the nativity. Oswald sat next to Betty's mother and Betty sat on the other side and about halfway through dinner the old lady punched him in the ribs and said, 'Ask me what time it is.'

'OK,' he said. 'What time is it?'

'Half past kissing time; time to kiss again!' she said, then screamed with laughter and continued to repeat it over and over until Betty had to get up and take her home. It seems Miss Alma had gotten into the leaded eggnog.

Oswald had just dropped whipped cream from the sweet potato pie all down the front of his tie when Dottie Nivens, the president of the association, made an announcement. 'Before we start the program this evening, we have a first-time visitor with us tonight and I would like for him to stand up and tell us a little bit about himself.' Everyone clapped and they all turned around and smiled at him and sat waiting for him to speak.

Oswald's ears turned as red as the bells on the wall. Frances, seeing how uncomfortable he was, quickly stood up and said, 'Keep your seat, Mr. Campbell. Mr. Campbell is my guest tonight, and I can tell you he came all the way down here from Chicago to get away from bad old cold weather and to spend the winter with us and maybe longer, if we don't run him off with all our crazy doings.' They all laughed. 'So welcome to the community, Mr. Campbell.' They all clapped again and he made an attempt at a nod.

The program for the evening was a reading of ' 'Twas the Night Before Christmas' by Dottie Nivens, an unfortunate selection for a woman with a lisp, followed by a solo rendition of 'Rudolph the Red-Nosed Reindeer' played on the musical saw, and ending with a visit from Santa Claus, who came in the room with a large sack thrown over his shoulder.

Santa sat in the front and called out the names of the children in the room, and one by one each went up for their present. Oswald noticed that when they got back to the table and opened their packages, they all seemed to like what they got. After everyone had received gifts, Santa Claus stood up and said, 'Well, that's all, boys and girls.' But then, as he lifted his sack, he

74

pretended to find just one more present. 'Oh, wait a minute,' he said. 'Here's another one.' He read the card, looked out, and asked, 'Is there a little boy here named Oswald T. Campbell?' Everybody laughed and pointed. 'Come on up, Oswald,' said Santa. When he got there Oswald saw it was Claude Underwood under the beard, who asked, 'Have you been a good boy?' Oswald laughed and said he had, received his present, and went back to his seat.

The evening ended with the lighting of the tree. As soon as everyone was outside they all mashed together in a large clump, and Oswald found himself in the middle. He could not help but think about the photo in the old hotel brochure of those thirty people standing under a rosebush. People in Alabama must love to stand around in clumps. Butch Mannich was stationed in the doorway. When the children, standing over to the side mashed together in their own smaller clump, started singing 'O Christmas Tree,' he switched on the lights and they all applauded.

After it was over, Oswald walked home with Frances and Mildred. He told them the most amazing thing about the evening to him, besides all the food, was that all the kids seemed to love their presents. He said he almost never liked what he had gotten for Christmas. They smiled and explained that the reason they were all so pleased was because each year Dottie Nivens, the postmistress, opened the letters they had written to Santa Claus and told their parents exactly what they wanted. As they walked farther up the street, Oswald noticed that one side of the sky seemed to be glowing red off in the distance. Frances told him it was caused by the fires the Creoles lit along the riverbanks every Christmas Eve to light up the night for 'Poppa Christmas' and help him find his way to the homes of the Creole children. 'We used to go and watch him come up the river, but we don't go over there anymore,' she said.

Although it was around ten o'clock, the night was still mild and it was very pleasant with the moonlight shining through the trees, walking past all the houses with their Christmas lights twinkling in the windows. As they strolled along in silence listening to the night birds singing, Oswald suddenly began to experience an unfamiliar feeling he could not quite identify. He was actually glad he had gone to the dinner; it had not been that bad after all.

When he got home, Betty, who was downstairs in her nightgown with cold cream on her face, said, 'You don't have to worry about waking Mother up tonight, she's as drunk as a skunk and out like a light, so maybe I'll finally get some rest.'

When he got upstairs to his room, he unwrapped his present and saw that it was a brand-new hardcover copy of *Birds of Alabama*. It was signed *Merry Christmas, from the Lost River Community Association*. It was just what he wanted. And he had not even written Santa a letter.

★ ★ ★

76

The gift was really from Claude and Roy. A few days before Christmas, Claude had told Roy he felt sorry for Mr. Campbell.

'Why?'

'Aw, the poor guy, he comes down to that dock waiting for the mail, and all he ever gets is some pension check from the government. The whole time he's been here, he hasn't received one personal letter, not even one lousy Christmas card.'

What they did not know was that Oswald did not expect to receive any mail. He was down at the dock every day only because he did not have anywhere else to go, except to the store and back to his room again. All he was doing was just sitting around killing time, looking at the birds and waiting to die.

Being aware that his days were numbered was not easy. Oswald found the hardest part was to wake up each morning with nothing to look forward to but getting worse. From what the doctor had told him, Oswald had assumed that as time passed he would start to feel weaker and weaker. However, on December 31 he woke up and noticed he was not coughing as much as he used to. He was really starting to feel pretty good, and somehow for the first time in his life, certainly for the first time since he was fifteen, he had actually managed to get through Christmas sober. In the past he had never been able to get more than one year in AA because he could never make it through the holidays without falling off the wagon, usually on Christmas Day. And also for the first time, he was experiencing another unfamiliar feeling. He was proud of himself and wished he had someone to tell. Not only had he made it through Christmas, he had also put on about five extra pounds since he had been there and he noticed in the mirror that he had a lot more color in his cheeks. This place was obviously agreeing with him. Damn, he thought. If he hadn't known better he could have sworn he *was* better.

On New Year's Day, Frances and Betty and everybody up and down the street made him come in, and they all insisted that he eat a big bowl of black-eyed peas. They said it was good luck to eat them on New Year's Day, and by that night he was up to his ears in black-eyed peas. Maybe they were right. Maybe he would get lucky and last a little longer than he had expected.

A few mornings later when Oswald sat down for breakfast, Betty announced, 'Well, Mr. Campbell, you're famous. You've made the papers,' and she handed him a copy of the local newsletter that came out once a month.

ALONG THE RIVER

The Lost River
Community Association Newsletter

Oh, my, what a busy and happy Christmas season we had on the river! Everyone agreed that the 'Mystery Tree' was prettier than ever this year. Kudos to those secret elves, who must have come down from the North

Pole to surprise us yet again! If we only knew who they were we would thank them in person.

Christmas Eve Dinner was especially delicious. We are mightily blessed with an abundance of good cooks down here and mucho thanks to the good ladies and gents who made the hall so festive and so full of Christmas cheer. A special nod goes to Sybil Underwood, who supplied the centerpieces; we are all amazed at what she can do with only simple pinecones and a few sprigs of holly. Thanks also to husband Claude for the fried mullet. Yum, yum. We had the largest crowd ever and it was good to see Betty Kitchen's mother, Miss Alma, out and about again. As usual, the highlight of the evening for the children was a visit by good old Santa Claus himself. All the boys and girls loved their presents, including our newest member, Mr. Oswald T. Campbell. Welcome!

The evening ended as usual with the annual tree-lighting ceremony, and amid the oohs and ahhs of the crowd I heard someone say that those folks up at Rockefeller Center in New York have nothing on us. I could not agree more.

And so ends another Christmas season, with all of us worn down to a frazzle and exhausted from all the busy activity but already looking forward to next year's happy Noel. In the meantime, all you lovebirds out there, married or single, don't forget to grab *your sweetheart for the annual Valentine's Dinner on February 14. Yours truly and Frances Cleverdon will be the hostesses again this year, and we promise that love will definitely be in the air!*

— Dottie Nivens

After he finished reading, Betty said, 'You know, Mr. Campbell, Dottie's no stranger to the written word. When she was younger she had herself quite a little literary fling up there in Manhattan.'

'Is that so?' he said, although he was not surprised. She certainly did look the artistic type, since she usually wore a long black scarf and a black velvet beret on her head.

'Oh, yes,' said Betty. 'She lived in Greenwich Village and was a genuine bohemian, from what I understand. Dottie told me she thought she was going to be the next Edna Ferber or Pearl Buck, but it didn't work out so she had to get a job.'

'That's too bad,' he said.

'Yes, but she's a good sport about it. When Dottie became our official postmistress she said she'd always hoped she'd wind up a woman of letters, but this was not quite what she had in mind.'

Oswald understood how she felt. He had always dreamed of becoming an architect someday but instead wound up working as a draftsman all his life. His ambitions had never quite panned out either. He might have a lot more in common with her than he had thought,

80

which would please Frances. Although Oswald did not know it, in her secret scheme to get him married, Dottie Nivens was second in line to get him if he and Mildred did not work out. And at the moment that did not seem to be going anywhere, at least as far as she could glean from Mildred. After that first dinner with Oswald at her house she had tried her best to get at least a clue as to how she felt. After he had left that night she had asked Mildred, 'Well, what do you think?' Mildred had looked at her as if she had no idea what she meant. 'About what?' She knew full well what Frances had meant and was just being cantankerous to irritate her. But far be it from Mildred to tell you what she was really thinking!

★　★　★

Sunday mornings in Lost River were quiet. Almost everyone, including Betty Kitchen and her mother, went over to the little town of Lillian for church. Frances and Mildred had asked Oswald to go with them, but he was not a churchgoing man. Another person who did not go was Claude Underwood, who went fishing. When asked why, he told everyone that he attended the Church of the Speckled Trout and would much rather be on the river than be in a suit and tie cooped up in some hot stuffy building.

One Sunday in early January, Claude rode by the dock, noticed Oswald sitting there in his chair with his book, and pulled over to him.

'I see the girls haven't drug you off to Lillian with them,' Claude said, smiling.

'No, they tried, but I escaped.'

'What are you doing?'

'Oh, nothing, just looking.'

'Then why don't you come fishing with me?'

'I don't know how to fish. Could I just tag along for the ride?'

'Sure, get in.'

It was a clear bright blue morning and the sun sparkled on the water as Claude rode all the way up to the wide part of the river. Flocks of pelicans flew beside the boat, almost close enough to reach out and touch. While they were sitting in the middle, the river was so still and peaceful; the only sound was the faint whirring of Claude's fishing reel and the soft *plop* as the lure hit the water. Oswald was amazed at the ease and grace with which Claude cast his line out and drew it back, with almost no effort.

While they were sitting there in the quiet, Oswald heard church bells ringing way off in the distance. He asked Claude where they were coming from.

'That's the Creole church across the river. You can hear it sometimes if the wind is right.' He laughed. 'Sometimes on Saturday night you can hear them playing their music, whooping and hollering and carrying on. They like to have a good time, I'll say that for them.'

'Do any of the Creoles ever come over to our side of the river?'

Claude sighed. 'They used to, but not anymore.'

'What are they like?'

'Most of them are as nice as you could want, would give you the shirt off their backs. I had a lot of good Creole friends at one time, but after that thing with Roy and Julian we just don't mix. After that happened everybody was more or less forced to take sides. Since the Creoles are all pretty much related to one another they had to side with Julian whether they agreed with him or not, and all of us over here had to do the same. It's sort of a Hatfield and McCoy kind of a thing, I guess. We don't go over there; they don't come over here.'

Oswald, curious, asked, 'What happened?'

'Didn't the women tell you about it?'

'No.'

Claude threw his line out in the water and began to reel it back in. 'Well, back about seventeen or maybe eighteen years by now we had ourselves a real-life Romeo and Juliet situation, and it's a dang miracle somebody wasn't murdered over it. It was touch and go there for a long time, with threats going back and forth across the river. Roy swore he was going to kill Julian and Julian swore he was going to kill Roy, and to this day there's still a lot of bad blood between them. I think if either one of them got caught on the wrong side of the river, look out.'

Roy seemed like such an even-tempered man to Oswald. 'Do you really think Roy would kill him?'

'You better believe it. Julian would do the same if he got the chance, and it's a damn shame, too. Roy was practically raised by Julian and thought the world of him until that mess over Julian's daughter. I don't know the exact details of what happened, but the women do. I'm sure there is right and wrong on both sides, but I do think Julian's pride caused most of the trouble.'

'Really?'

'Oh, yeah, back in the seventeen hundreds the LaPonde family used to own all of Baldwin County all the way up to Mobile. Julian's great-grandfather got the original land grant from the king of Spain, but over the years the family sold most of it off bit by bit, got cheated out of some of it, lost a lot of it in poker games, and eventually wound up with just the land on the other side of the river.'

A small boat came around the corner and two men waved at Claude. 'Having any luck?'

Claude waved back. 'Not much,' he said as they went by. 'Anyhow, about sixty years ago some of the farmers that came down to Baldwin County and bought land thought the Creoles were just a little too dark for their tastes and also they were Catholic and did their share of drinking and that didn't set too well with the farmers, so there was some talk about maybe they shouldn't be going to the same schools as their children and evidently there was going to be some sort of vote, but Julian's father got wind of it and he pulled all the Creoles out of the county school and started one of their own. Julian was just a kid then, and he swore that when he grew up he was going to get his family's

84

original Spanish land grant back and kick the farmers off their land or some such crazy idea. He wanted his daughter, Marie, to marry the Voltaire boy so he could get some of the LaPonde land back in the family, but Marie wanted to marry Roy. As I say, I don't know what all took place, but after it was over the girl wound up marrying the Voltaire boy and Roy ran off and joined the marines.'

Oswald had not been aware that Claude had hooked something while he was talking, but at that moment Claude casually reached over and pulled a mean-looking fish with a long skinny snout full of teeth out of the water and into the boat.

'What is *that*?' asked Oswald, moving aside.

'This old boy is a gar, puts up a nice little fight but not good to eat,' he said, unhooking the fish. Putting him back in the water he said, 'Sorry, fella.'

★ ★ ★

The next week, when Oswald went over to have dinner with Frances and Mildred again, he asked Frances about the feud between Roy and Julian LaPonde.

Frances looked at him. 'Oh, Mr. Campbell, you don't even want to know about that; it was just terrible. I just don't want to tell you how awful it was.' She then sat down on the couch and proceeded to tell him the entire story. 'When that mess was going on, Ralph, my poor husband, had to get up and go down there in the middle of the night and help try and stop Roy from going across the river and killing Julian. And evidently, from what I heard, his relatives had to hold Julian back from coming over here and killing Roy. Julian accused Roy of ruining his girl's reputation or some such nonsense and said he was going to shoot him if he got the chance. Ralph said poor Roy was down at the store having a fit, he was so in love with Marie LaPonde, and you can't blame him; she was a beautiful girl. But then, as mean as he was, Julian was always a good-looking man, you have to say that for him don't you, Mildred?'

Mildred, who tonight had black hair with a white streak down the middle, said, 'I don't know. I never saw the man.'

'Oh, that's right,' said Frances. 'You weren't here yet, but he was as good-looking as a movie star with those blue-green eyes; all the women were crazy about him. Anyhow, Roy and Marie had practically grown up together and had been in love with each other since they were children. So when he was eighteen, Roy told Julian that he and Marie wanted to get married, and Julian had a fit and said no, absolutely not, that the only way Roy could marry Marie was over his dead body. Marie's mother, who loved Roy like a son, begged Julian to change his mind, and so did Roy's uncle, who was his good friend, but he would not budge. He claimed he was against it because Roy was not Catholic, but the truth was Julian wanted that Voltaire land back and the only way he could get his hands on it was to have Marie marry into the family. So when all else

86

failed Roy somehow got a note to Marie and rowed over there late one night to get her so they could run off and get married, but Julian caught them just as they were leaving the dock and drug Marie out of the boat and shot at Roy. Oh, it was terrible. People said they heard poor Marie screaming and crying and pleading with her father all the way across the river. The very next day Julian took Marie off and stuck her in a convent somewhere where Roy couldn't find her.'

Mildred said, 'Why didn't she just leave? That's what I would have done.'

'I don't think it was that easy, Mildred. I think she was afraid her father would hurt Roy, or maybe being a good Catholic girl she felt obligated to do what he said, but anyway about a year later she managed to get a letter to Roy and told him she had decided to go ahead and marry the Voltaire boy. And do you know what the worst part of this story is?'

Mildred, who had already knocked back two vodka martinis, said, 'That the dinner is getting cold.'

Frances ignored her sister and continued. 'The worst part is after all that, the Voltaire boy lost all his family's land gambling, and he and Marie had to move to Louisiana. So Julian broke two hearts and destroyed two lives, all for naught. It's a real-life tragedy so we just don't talk about it. Especially to Roy. I know he's still in love with her.'

Mildred turned to Oswald. 'It sounds like the plot of a really bad novel, doesn't it?'

You should know, thought Frances, as she stood up to go to the kitchen, but she did not say it. She did not want Mr. Campbell to know what kind of junk her sister read and wished Mildred could be more like Dottie Nivens, who at least aspired to better herself. She read great literature, Chaucer, Proust, and Jane Austen, not those cheap romance novels Mildred always picked. As she pulled the roast out of her pink stove she also wondered why Mildred had worn that low-cut blouse that showed the top of her more than generous where-withals. Was she interested in Mr. Campbell? Or was she just not paying attention to what she put on? With Mildred you never knew.

A Small Visitor

One afternoon Oswald was standing around the cash register talking with Roy, when Roy suddenly picked up a pencil, pretended to be writing something, and said, 'Don't look now, but that little girl I was telling you about is back.'

The first time Roy had seen the little girl was a few weeks before, and then it was only the top of a small blonde head slowly rising up and appearing in the side window, then two big wide blue eyes staring in at Jack running on his plastic wheel and ringing his bells. But the minute she saw Roy she quickly disappeared from sight. Roy walked back and went outside, but by the time he got around the side of the building she was nowhere to be seen. He had noticed her only a few times, but it was always the same; as soon as she saw him looking at her, she disappeared into thin air.

The next time she came he was able to catch sight of her before she saw him. He quickly turned his back and pretended not to notice her. From what he had seen of her, she was a pretty little thing, and was clearly shy and afraid of people, but obviously fascinated with the bird. She came every day after that, and Roy got a big kick out of it.

'Who is she?' asked Oswald, not turning around.

'I don't know. I've asked Frances and Dottie, but nobody knows who she is or where she came from. I just wish I could get her to come in.'

★   ★   ★

As the days went by the girl became bolder and bolder, until one afternoon when Roy opened the back door she did not run away. 'Don't you want to come inside?' he said. 'He can't come out, but if you come in you can pet him if you want. He doesn't mind.'

Roy, seeing how small she was, guessed the girl could not have been more than five or six. She was barefoot and wearing a dirty ripped cotton dress, and she stood there, clearly torn between being terrified of Roy and wanting to see Jack up close.

'Come on in,' he said. 'Nobody's going to hurt you.' The girl started to turn around and leave but Roy said, 'Wait a minute, don't go,' and went back in and picked Jack up and held his feet between his forefinger and thumb and walked to the door so she could see him. 'Look. You can hold him if you want. He's tame, he won't hurt you.'

Jack looked at her through the screen and sang out, 'Chip, chip, chip, birdie, birdie, birdie.'

After a moment the girl could not resist and slowly began to move toward the door. It was then Roy noticed that there was something wrong with her. As she came closer and closer he

90

could see that her body was slightly twisted and she was dragging her right leg behind her. 'What's your name?' he asked as she came in, with her eyes never leaving Jack.

She answered 'Patsy' so softly he could barely hear her.

'Well, Patsy. This is Jack.'

It had been Roy's experience that at first most children this young were afraid to touch the bird, but not her. She may have been frightened of people but not of Jack. She said, 'Can I hold him?'

'Sure.'

She lifted her finger and held it up, and Jack walked from Roy's finger over to hers and sat there cocking his head and blinking his eyes. Usually in the past when he had put Jack on someone else's finger, he had always hopped right back to him. Not this time.

'He likes you,' said Roy.

Her eyes were wide with wonder. 'He does?' she said.

'Oh, yes.' At that point Jack bobbed up and down on her finger and walked all the way up her arm, sat on her shoulder, and nuzzled against the side of her cheek. 'Well, I'll be darned,' said Roy.

This was the beginning of the love affair between Jack and Patsy.

★   ★   ★

When Patsy left the store that first day, Roy walked out and watched where she was headed.

He finally figured out where she lived and why nobody in town knew who she was. She had headed in the same direction where those people who lived way back up in the woods were located. She probably belonged to the same family as the two mean boys who had shot Jack in the first place, and most likely had heard about the bird from them. He remembered the first day she had appeared was the same day he had seen those boys walk by the store and look in at Jack. What a shame, thought Roy; he could just imagine what kind of life she had. But all he could do was to be as nice as possible to her while she was here. The kind of people who lived back there in the woods never stayed anywhere long. They were mostly itinerant farm workers passing through the area to pick strawberries or work the pecan crop and then move on to the next place.

After that first time, the girl came back to the store every day and played with Jack for hours. She was still terrified of people and shy with Roy, although he found she was no trouble to have around. She was as quiet as a mouse. The only time he ever heard her at all was when she was alone in the office with Jack. If he happened to pass by, he could hear her in there, just chattering away to the bird — and darned if the bird wasn't chattering back at her. He would have loved to hear what she was saying, but he couldn't make it out. As the weeks went by she got to the point where she would come out of the office and talk to people. When Roy first introduced her to Oswald, who was not very comfortable around children, he awkwardly reached down and shook her hand and said, 'Hello little girl, how do you do,' and was amazed at her tiny hand. As she walked away and he saw how badly crippled she was, he turned to Roy and said softly, 'That's a damn shame. She's such a pretty little kid, too.'

Roy glanced back as she went into the office. 'Yeah, it makes you want to kick the living tar out of somebody, don't it?'

The next time Oswald came up to the store, he saw Patsy in the back and she shyly motioned for him to come over. 'Do you want to know a secret?' she asked.

'Why, yes, I do.'

She then motioned for him to lean down and whispered in his ear. 'Jack is my best friend.'

'Really?' he said, pretending to be astonished. 'How do you know?' he whispered back.

'He told me.'

'He did? And what did you say?'

'I told him first and then he told me.'

'I see.'

'But he said I could tell you.'

'Well, tell him I said thank you.'

'OK,' she said.

When he walked over to the cash register he was laughing to himself. 'Hey, Roy, did you know she's back there, talking to that bird?'

'Oh, yes, I hear her all day, just chattering away, lost in her own world. But you know what, considering what she must go home to every night, the kid probably needs some magic in her

93

life. She can stay back there forever, as far as I'm concerned.'

Of course, when Frances and the other women saw the girl they were appalled, not only at her condition but also at how thin and dirty she was. Butch Mannich got mad and fumed over it. He had no patience with that kind of child neglect. Being a process server he had dealt firsthand with the type of people that lived back in the woods and knew what they were like. He said, 'They treat their kids worse than you and I would treat a dog.'

From then on, every time Frances went in the store the sight of the girl broke her heart. She told Roy, 'I'm just worried to death about her, and you just wonder what her mother must be like, to let a crippled child roam around like some wild animal. Somebody ought to do something.'

'I know, Frances,' said Roy, shaking his head. 'I've tried to feed her but she won't take a thing from me but a few pieces of candy. All she wants is to play with Jack all day. I feel bad for her, but she doesn't belong to us and there's nothing we can do about it.'

Something New

As the days went by, Patsy charmed everyone who met her. Even Oswald found that now when he went to the store he was looking forward to visiting with Patsy as much as anything else. As a matter of fact, after a while he realized much to his amazement that he was crazy about the little girl. She was the first and only child he had ever liked. He had mostly always been around boys, so he figured it must be because she *was* a girl, so tiny and frail. Or maybe it was that he felt a kinship with Patsy — and Jack, too, for that matter. They were all three handicapped in one way or another. He went up to the store one morning as usual and when he got there she was in the back office playing with Jack.

'How are you today, Patsy?'

'Fine.'

'What are you up to?'

'Nothing. Jack and I are just playing.'

She was busy pretending to serve tea to Jack and offered Oswald a cup of imaginary tea.

'Hey, Patsy, how old are you?' he asked.

'I don't know.'

'Well, when is your next birthday?'

She thought about it. 'I don't know. I don't think I have one.'

'You don't have a birthday?'

'No.'

He took another cup of imaginary tea from her and pretended to drink it. 'You know what? You're not going to believe this, but I don't have a birthday either. I have an idea. Let's you and I make one up. Then every year you and I will have the same birthday, OK? And we won't tell anybody; it will be our secret.'

'OK,' she said.

He looked at the calendar on the wall. 'How about Wednesday, three days from now?'

'Can it be Jack's birthday, too?'

'I don't see why not.'

'OK,' she said, and they shook hands.

The next day, Oswald asked Butch if he could get a ride over to Lillian. Never having bought a present for a child before, he was at a loss. He wandered around the general merchandise store in the small town, looking for something she might like. He didn't know how to pick out a doll, or what kind of toys girls played with, but then he spotted a black beanie decorated with Dr Pepper bottle caps.

Wednesday came, and they had their secret birthday back in the office. He gave her the hat and she gave him two pieces of candy she had saved and wrapped up in brown paper and string. She was as thrilled with her hat as he hoped she would be. Oswald sat there eating the candy and drinking more imaginary tea and watching Jack peck away at his present of sunflower seeds. Then he remarked, 'You know, Patsy, this is the best birthday I ever had.'

She sat across from him wearing her new Dr Pepper hat and declared, 'Me too!'

After a while Oswald had another idea and went out to the cash register.

'Hey, Roy, do you have a camera?'

'Yeah.'

'Can I borrow it? I want to take a picture of Patsy.'

'Sure, let me put some film in and we'll do it.'

After some time deciding where the best light was, they stood Patsy outside the front door of the store and took her picture, holding Jack and wearing her new beanie. A week later, Oswald brought the finished black-and-white photo and showed it to her. He had had three copies made, one for Roy and one for Patsy and one to keep for himself. Roy taped his photo to the side of the cash register so everyone who came in could see it. Across the bottom was written *Patsy and Jack on their birthday*.

A Dilemma

One February morning Roy came in the store and whistled for Jack, but the bird did not answer. He whistled again. No answer. He looked around the store and wondered what the crazy thing was into today when he suddenly saw a large man's work glove walking across the top of the lettuce and across the lemons. During the night Jack had somehow gotten himself tangled up inside the glove and could not get out. Roy went over and pulled it off. Jack was all ruffled up and mad; he must have been in there for hours. He shook his feathers and stomped all over the lemons and slipped in between two of them and got even madder. Roy laughed at him. 'You nutty bird, you.' Always getting himself in trouble. Last week he had caught him pecking holes in all the tomatoes and later that day when Mildred had come in she had screamed bloody murder. 'There's not one good tomato here!' she said. 'How can a person be expected to make a decent salad as long as that horrible little bird is around?'

Jack responded by running around on his wheel and ringing his bells, almost as if he were laughing at Mildred. Roy thought it was hilarious but Mildred was not amused.

★　★　★

Oswald had recently started getting up at daybreak and was usually down at the store by seven to have a cup of coffee with Roy before going out on the river. But the next morning Oswald seemed flushed and was already banging at the window at six-thirty. Roy walked over and opened the door. 'Oh, hell, let me in,' Oswald said, and ran into the store.

'What's the matter?'

'Man, I'm in trouble,' he said, holding up an envelope. 'Betty, Mildred, Frances, and now Dottie Nivens have all asked me to this Valentine thing over at the hall, and I don't know what to do. Oh, man,' he said, wringing his hands. 'These women are going to drive me to drink.'

'Well, which lucky lady are you going to go with?'

'It doesn't matter. Whoever I pick, the other three are going to be mad at me.'

Roy thought about it. 'If I were you I would explain it to Frances and let them fight it out among themselves.'

After he left, Roy had to smile. Oswald was certainly the most unlikely Lothario he had ever seen.

Oswald could not have agreed with him more. He had never been asked out on a date in his life, much less by four women on the same night. Reluctantly he explained the situation to Frances.

As it turned out, all four had invited him because they wanted to make sure he would not feel left out and did not know the others had done the same. And so it was decided that all four women were to be his date.

99

★ ★ ★

On Valentine's night poor Oswald, wearing a red bow tie and even though he was a terrible dancer, had to dance every dance. He waltzed with Frances to a sappy version of 'Dreamy Alabama,' jitterbugged with Dottie Nivens, did some odd tango thing with Mildred, and ended the evening being dragged around the floor by his six-foot landlady to the tune of 'Good Night Sweetheart.'

ALONG THE RIVER

The Lost River
Community Association Newsletter

Oh, what a delightful evening was had by all who attended the annual Sweethearts dance! The melodious tunes that had all of our toes literally dancing inside our shoes was supplied by the ever-popular Auburn Knights Swing Band, and we were all mighty impressed by their musicality and wide range of repertoire, from the fox-trot to the jazzy idioms and interpolations of the bossa nova. But the highlight of the evening was the nimble Terpsichore of our own Fred Astaire in the person of Oswald T. Campbell, who if I may borrow a phrase was truly the belle of the ball!

After Oswald read that first paragraph and later when Roy and Claude started calling him

100

Belle, he decided that all of this female attention was making him a nervous wreck. He had so many dinner invitations he had to write them down.

He needed to get to an AA meeting fast.

Butch Mannich knew a lot of people in the nearby towns, so the next time Oswald saw him walking up the street he stopped him and asked if he by any chance knew anyone in AA.

Butch brightened up. 'Yes, by gosh, I sure do. I know a man over in Elberta who belongs. I didn't know you were in that, Mr. Campbell.'

'Yes,' said Oswald, 'but it's not something I'm particularly proud of, and I would appreciate it if you could sort of keep it under your hat. I don't want anybody to know, especially Frances.'

Butch nodded and conspired in a whisper. 'I understand completely, Mr. Campbell, and I don't blame you, but don't you worry. Your secret is safe with me. I won't say a word to anybody.' Butch glanced around to see if anyone was looking and quickly wrote a name and number down on a piece of paper. He looked around again to make sure no one saw him and then slipped him the piece of paper on the sly.

Oswald called the number that afternoon, and a man answered.

'Is this Mr. Krause?'

'That's me.'

'Mr. Krause, I was given your number by Butch Mannich over in Lost River.'

'You mean Stick?'

'Yes, sir.'

'Well, any friend of Stick's is a friend of mine.

What can I do for you?'

'Uh . . . I understand you are in AA, and I wanted to ask you when the next meeting was.' Mr. Krause told him there was a weekly meeting at eight o'clock on Friday nights at the Knights of Columbus hall in downtown Elberta and to please come. 'We will be glad to have you. We are always happy to have new members. Where are you from?'

'Chicago.'

Mr. Krause was impressed. 'Ah, Chicago. I bet there are a lot of great meetings up there. We are just a small group over here. Are you a beginner, Mr. Campbell, or have you been at it for a while?'

'No, I'm not a beginner, I have a few years, but I haven't been to a meeting in quite a while and you know once you stop going it's hard to start all over in a new town.'

'You got that right, Mr. Campbell. You have to keep coming or you get out of practice. But don't you worry, we'll get you right back in the swing in no time.'

'By the way, is this a men's meeting?' Oswald asked.

'We have one or two women but mostly men.'

Good, thought Oswald. It would be a nice break for him.

★ ★ ★

Friday night Butch said he would be glad to drive Oswald over to the meeting. He had some people he needed to see anyway, so they drove over before dark. Elberta was a small German farming community about ten miles to the east, and the houses had an almost Bavarian look to them. Butch took him to the Elks Club where he was a member and introduced him around to a few friends. Around seven-thirty after they had eaten hamburgers at the lodge, Butch drove him downtown, parked on a side street, and furtively glanced around in all directions to make sure the coast was clear before he let him out. 'I'll be back to get you in an hour,' he said.

Oswald asked if he could give him an hour and a half. 'Since this is my first meeting here, I'd like to try and get to know some of the fellows.'

'No problem,' said Butch. 'And don't you worry, Mr. Campbell, mum's the word.' And with that he sped off into the night.

Oswald went inside the large Knights of Columbus hall and found a sign that said ALABAMA AA with the arrow pointing upstairs. A heavyset man in suspenders greeted him with a big beefy handshake and a pat on the back that nearly knocked him down.

'Mr. Campbell? Ed Krause. Welcome to our little group.'

Oswald looked around the room. There were already six or seven other friendly-looking men sitting in wooden chairs, smiling and nodding at him.

Mr. Krause led him to a chair. 'Where's your instrument, Mr. Campbell?'

Oswald was not sure what he had heard. 'I beg your pardon?'

It was only when he looked around the room

again that he noticed that all the men were pulling accordions out of the cases beside each chair.

When another man walked by with a big black case and carrying an armload of sheet music, Oswald suddenly realized that he had walked into an Alabama Accordion Association meeting!

He turned to the man and said, 'Ah . . . I tell you what, Mr. Krause, I believe I'll just listen tonight. My instrument is sort of on the blink.'

'That's too bad,' said a disappointed Ed Krause. 'We were looking forward to a little new blood.'

Oswald went over in the corner and sat and listened. He sat through quite a few polkas and one pretty lively version of 'The Poor People of Paris' before it was time for Butch to come and pick him up. Outside, Butch asked how the meeting went and he answered, 'Just fine.'

On the way back home, Oswald thought about it and wondered which was worse, being an accordion player or being an alcoholic. He figured it was a toss-up.

★　★　★

He was sorry there were no AA meetings around, but Oswald figured he was doing pretty well just hanging out on the dock and meeting with the birds every day. It seemed to keep him calm, and it was certainly interesting. He was not bored. There were plenty of them to see. One day when Oswald was sitting there on the dock busy watching the birds, a great blue heron stared right back at him, and it suddenly occurred to him that they might be busy watching him as well. He wondered what they thought he was, and how would they identify him.

His *Birds of Alabama* book had given him guidelines as to how to identify birds by size and color and by location, so he decided to look in the book and figure out what the birds would write down for him. He searched for himself up under LOCATION:

PERMANENT RESIDENTS: Live in the same geographic region all year long.

SUMMER RESIDENTS: Breed and raise their young in one geographic region, then leave to winter in warmer regions.

WINTER VISITORS: Come to a geographic region only during winter months after their breeding season.

TRANSIENTS: Pass through a geographic region only once or twice a year during their spring or fall migrations.

ACCIDENTALS: Birds not expected in a particular region and, therefore, are surprise visitors.

As he read on, he decided that according to the book, he was definitely a medium-sized, redheaded, nonbreeding accidental. At last he knew what he was, and it amused him to no end. He was a rare bird, after all.

Winter

On the morning of February 21, everybody up and down the street declared, 'Well, winter is here,' and noted with horror that last night the temperature had dipped all the way down into the 50s. That afternoon, Oswald looked across the river and for the first time saw blue smoke curling out of the chimneys of the houses on the other side. The air was suddenly fragrant with the smell of wood smoke from the burning of local pine, hickory, and cedar logs.

Oswald welcomed the cooler weather because in the following days he discovered it brought winter sunsets, and the river sunsets were different from anything else he had ever seen. They mesmerized him. He loved sitting there on the dock in the cool crisp air, the river so quiet you could hear a dog bark a mile away. Every afternoon he watched the sky turn from burnt orange to salmon, pink and lime green to purple. Navy blue and pink clouds were reflected in the water, and as the sun slowly disappeared he watched the river change from teal blue to an iridescent green and gold that reminded him of the color of the tinfoil that came wrapped around expensive candy and then from rich tan to a deep chocolate brown. As the evening became darker, the birds and ducks that flew by became black silhouettes against the sky. He sat each night watching the evening change colors and the currents of the water make circles, until the moon came up behind him and rose over the river.

With the last of the sun fading, he could see the reflection of the green lights on the docks across the way and the stars twinkling in the river like small diamonds. What a show. This was better than any movie he had ever seen, and it was different every night. It was so wonderful at times he felt he wanted to do something about it, to try and stop time, make it last longer, but he didn't know what to do. How can anyone stop time? He knew with each passing day his own time was running out, and there was nothing anybody could do to stop it. If he could, he would have stopped it right then and there on the river, while he was still well enough to enjoy it.

★   ★   ★

A few weeks later, Oswald was still feeling well, and Jack was still making everyone laugh except Mildred, and everything was going along as usual until Saturday morning, when Patsy showed up at the store to see Jack. One side of her face was red, and it was obvious that someone had hit her. Roy asked her how it had happened, but she said nothing. Butch, who had been in the store first thing that morning, was in a rage over it. Afterward all six-feet-four-inches

107

and 128 pounds of him stormed down the street to Frances's house in a fit and threw open the door.

'That just aggravates the fire out of me!'

'What?' asked Frances.

'Somebody hit Patsy!'

'Who?'

'I don't know!'

'Are you sure?'

'Sure, I'm sure. There's a big old handprint on the side of her face.'

That afternoon an emergency meeting of the Mystic Order of the Royal Polka Dots secret society was called to discuss what could be done. After much talk back and forth, Betty Kitchen allowed that Roy might be right. She said, 'There may be nothing we can do without getting those people back there all riled up. You all know what they are like.'

Mildred said, 'Trailer trash.'

Frances said, 'Oh, now, Mildred, that's not a very Christian thing to say.'

'No,' said Mildred, 'but it's the truth.'

Butch admired her ability to hit the nail on the head. Frances got back to the point. 'Now, I think we all agree that this is definitely a Polka Dot matter, and I think the least we can do is offer to buy her some decent clothes. Here it is, the dead of winter, and the little thing is still running around with no coat or shoes.'

'How much money do we have in our Sunshine fund?' asked Betty.

Frances went over to her gravy boat display, and lifted the top off the third one from the left, and pulled out $82. They took a vote to spend it all on Patsy, and the motion passed unanimously.

Betty said, 'The next question is who and how are we going to ask the family if we can do it.'

Mildred said, 'Why don't we just take her to Mobile and do it ourselves? Why ask?'

Frances looked at her. 'We can't just take her, Mildred. They might have us all arrested for kidnapping. That's all we need is to go to jail.'

'Yes, but if you go back there where they live they're liable to turn the dogs on you,' warned Dottie. 'Or shoot you.'

'Well, two can play that game,' said Butch, patting the sidearm he wore under his shirt. 'They're not the only ones around here with guns, you know.'

'Oh, Lord,' said Frances. 'That's all we need is gunplay.'

'Why don't we go as a group?' asked Mildred.

Frances shook her head. 'No, that might be too threatening. I think one of us should just casually pay a visit like a friendly neighbor. Who wants to go?'

Butch raised his hand.

'No, not you, Butch, it has to be a woman,' said Mildred.

Betty Kitchen said, 'Well, I'll go. I'm not afraid of any man. They fool with me and I'll sling them into tomorrow and back.'

Dottie, who knew that Betty was not exactly capable of being subtle, said quickly, 'I think you should go, Frances. You're the nicest and least likely to get thrown out.'

★ ★ ★

The following Sunday, Frances parked her car at the store and walked down the white sandy path in her high heels, carrying a purse on one arm and a large welcome basket on the other, hoping she would live through the day. Throughout the years a variety of people had moved back up in the woods, and her husband had told her it was best to let them alone. Some were hiding from the law and were not very friendly to strangers. They usually stayed awhile, threw trash everywhere, and then moved on. A few years ago, the sheriff's department had arrested some of them, so there was no telling what she was walking into today. A few moments later she suddenly heard a loud crack, which almost scared her to death. She thought she had been shot. She turned to see Butch, who had been darting back and forth in the woods trailing behind her and had stepped on a branch. 'Oh, my God, Butch, what are you doing? You nearly gave me a heart attack!'

Still darting, he jumped behind a tree and said in a whisper, 'Don't worry about me, you just go on. I'm here just in case you need me.'

Oh, Lord, she thought. Butch had clearly seen too many movies. She continued on until she reached a clearing and saw a broken-down trailer sitting up on concrete blocks. An old rusted ice box lay on its side in the yard, along with an assortment of worn tires and motorcycle and car parts. As she got closer, some kind of pit-bull-mix dog came rushing toward her, barking furiously, baring his teeth, and straining

110

at his chain. Frances stopped dead in her tracks. In a moment a five-foot-tall fat woman in a tank top and short shorts opened the door, yelled at the dog to shut up, and then saw Frances standing there.

'Hello,' said Frances, trying to sound casual, 'I hope I'm not bothering you. I'm Mrs. Frances Cleverdon, and I was wondering if I might speak to you for a moment.'

The woman stared at her. 'If you're a bill collector, it won't do you no good. My husband ain't here.'

Frances, trying to reassure her, said, 'Oh, no, I'm just a neighbor lady come to chat and bring you a little gift.'

The woman shifted her small pig eyes to the basket. 'You wanna come in?'

'Yes, thank you.' Frances climbed the concrete steps while the dog leaped up and down and literally foamed at the mouth. The place was a mess. She took note of the empty beer cans on the counter and a box of stale doughnuts. The woman sat down and crossed her enormous white leg with the tattoo of a snake around her equally enormous ankle. After Frances had moved a few things and made a place to sit, she said, 'I'm sorry, I don't know your name.'

'Tammie Suggs.'

'Well, Mrs. Suggs, I really came here today to discuss your little girl.'

The woman's eyes narrowed. 'What about her, what did she do? Patsy!' she yelled. 'Get out here!'

'No, that's all right, she didn't do anything — '

'If she stole something, I ain't paying for it.'

Patsy appeared from the back of the trailer, looking frightened.

'No. It's nothing like that, Mrs. Suggs. Hello, Patsy,' she said, and smiled.

Frances leaned forward. 'I was hoping we could speak in private.'

The woman turned and said to Patsy, 'Get out of here.'

Frances waited until she was gone. 'Mrs. Suggs, it's just that I . . . well, a group of us, actually — have grown very fond of Patsy and wondered if you had had a doctor look at her lately?'

'What for?'

'Well, her condition — her leg?'

'Oh, yeah, she drags that thing bad, don't she. But she was already like that when her daddy left her here. She ain't even my kid. She was just dumped on me. I don't have no money for doctors for my own kids, much less her. Then after her daddy took off, I got stuck with her and the next thing I know my old man up and runs off, and me and them kids is about to starve to death.'

Tammie Suggs looked far from starving, but Frances refrained from comment and continued. 'Do you know what causes her to walk like that? Was it an accident of some kind?'

Tammie Suggs shook her head. 'Naw, he told me it happened when she was born. Her mother was real delicate-like and was having a hard time delivering, so the doctor jerked her out with forceps, and it left her all twisted like that.'

112

'Oh, no!'

'Yeah. And the mother died anyway.'

'I see. Did he say if anything could be done about it, maybe special shoes of some kind?' Frances said, as a subtle hint.

Tammie shook her head and scratched her large arm. 'Naw, her daddy said she's always gonna be like that. That there weren't no use to put shoes on her, she just ruins every pair, dragging that foot like she does.'

'And where is the father now?' asked Frances, trying her best to remain pleasant.

'I don't know, but he better get his butt back here soon. I'm tired of putting up with her.' Frances could not help herself and winced slightly at the last statement. Tammie saw it and snapped at her. 'Look, lady, I'm doing the best I can. You try raising three kids with no man.'

'Oh, I'm sure it's very difficult, but maybe we could help you buy Patsy a few things, maybe some toys or clothes?'

Tammie thought it over for a moment. 'Well, me and the boys needs things, too.'

After she could see that there was really no use to try and reason with her, Frances put the envelope with the money on the table and left. When she got outside she was so disgusted with the woman she didn't know what to do. She walked by the dog, who was having another jumping-up-and-down fit, straining to break free from its chain and eat her alive. Frances, a lady to the core, uncharacteristically turned on him and said, 'Oh, shut up, you!' Butch caught up with her halfway to the car and Frances, who

113

had never been able to have children of her own, said, 'What kind of a man would leave his child with that horrible woman? You just wonder what the Good Lord is thinking about when he gives people like that children.'

For the next week, everybody watched Patsy to see if she showed up in shoes or anything other than that old dress, but she never did.

* * *

Although Patsy had no new clothes, Frances was determined to make sure the little girl had at least one good meal a day. At twelve o'clock each day, she walked down to the store with a hot lunch and sat with her in the office while she ate it. At first, Patsy was shy and afraid to eat, but Frances, who had once been a schoolteacher, was finally able to convince her that it was all right, and pretty soon she had her talking a lot more. As she left one day, Frances told Roy, 'You know, that is the sweetest little girl. It's all I can do not to just pick her up and squeeze her to death. Can you imagine a father leaving a child like that?'

Roy shook his head. 'No, I can't.' Then he said sadly, 'You know, Frances, there are a lot of people that should be shot.'

* * *

Roy would have shot Julian LaPonde a long time ago, if he had not been Marie's father and if her mother had not begged him not to. He was not

114

over Marie yet and still remembered how she looked that night, the last time he ever saw her.

He still wondered how she was doing. He could have found out from her mother, who liked him, or gone through the Catholic priest on the sly, but it would have been painful to know she had forgotten him and equally painful to know she had not. In her last letter to him, she had said that if he loved her he would forget her and find someone else and have a happy life. He loved her, all right, but have a happy life without her? That was something he had not been able to do.

Roy and Mildred had a lot in common. Mildred, although not as young as she used to be, still had a good figure, small hips, and large full breasts and years ago could have had any boy in Chattanooga but instead she had thrown her life away over Billy Jenkins. Why she had picked him over all the other boys that were lining up at her door was beyond Frances. He was certainly not up to her. A no-good lazy bum from the wrong side of the tracks, as their father had put it, but nothing would do at the time than for Mildred to settle on the one boy nobody in the family liked. Frances suspected that if they had liked him, Mildred would not have wanted to marry him. It was as if Mildred went out of her way to find the one unsuitable boy in town and go after him. It had been a small scandal and had cost their father a small fortune. The bridesmaids' dresses had been bought and fitted, the country club rented, food ordered, and invitations sent, and one week before the wedding the groom skipped town on a motorcycle, leaving a note saying *Sorry, I guess I wasn't ready. Love, Billy.* Mildred had been inconsolable and heartbroken for years. But Frances wondered if it was not so much over love as it was that Mildred always wanted what she couldn't have. Mildred had had a few men friends after that, but she never really loved any of them. None could ever compete with the one that got away.

An Awakening

Spring came to Lost River around the middle of March. The nights were slowly becoming warmer, and each evening as the sun went down, the mullet started jumping and splashing around in the river, almost as if they too were happy spring was here. Soon all the flowers Oswald had not seen when he arrived began to bloom. Almost overnight, the entire area was heady with the smell of gardenias, azaleas, wisteria, night-blooming jasmine, and honeysuckle. Oswald thought, if this were to be his last spring on earth, it was certainly the most spectacular one he had ever witnessed.

A few weeks later, on one balmy night as Oswald walked down the street, he saw fireflies flitting in and out of the bushes, and the wind blowing the Spanish moss through the trees forming shadows on the road. As he reached the river, Oswald suddenly felt as if he were walking around in a painting. Then it dawned on him. Everywhere he looked was a painting! Everything was alive with color: the water, the sky, the boathouses that lined the river, with red tin roofs, silver tin roofs, and rusted orange tin roofs. Red boat in a yellow boathouse. Green, pink, blue, tan, yellow, and white boathouses. The wooden pilings sticking out of the water were a thousand different shades of gray, and each individual piling was encrusted with hundreds of chalk-white barnacles and black woodpecker holes. Even the grain of the wood and the knots on each post differed from inch to inch and pole to pole. Vibrant color everywhere he looked and it all changed from season to season, from minute to minute. At that moment he thought, God, if he could only paint all the beautiful things he saw! He could live a thousand years and never run out of things to paint. Birds, trees, ducks, flowers. After Oswald had gotten out of the army, he had signed up for a course in architecture, but he never finished it. He had certainly never painted anything in his life, but when he had been younger, before he made a career out of drinking, he had always been tempted by those DRAW ME advertisements in magazines. One time he had gone so far as to actually send one in and they had written back and told him in glowing terms that he had talent and invited him to send off for a series of art courses, taught by famous artists, but Helen had discouraged him. She said it was just a scam and that they told everybody they had talent just to get you to buy lessons — so he had not followed up. But now he wondered if maybe they had been right. Maybe he might have talent. He could try a few things on his own; after all, he didn't have a thing to lose.

The next day he started by just doing the

black silhouettes of the birds and trees in pen and ink on the backs of old paper sacks, and after a week or two he had about ten drawings he thought were not half bad. He even gave one a name, 'The Lone Duck,' and signed it *O. T. Campbell*. A few weeks later he strolled around the store to the area where Roy kept the school supplies, picked up a long black tin box of watercolors, and asked Roy how much it was. 'A buck,' Roy said. 'OK,' he said, pulled out a dollar, and left. Roy thought he had bought the watercolors for Patsy, but he was wrong. Oswald felt a little foolish dipping his brush into paint shaped like stars and half moons, but he had to start somewhere and he needed to get as much practice as he could.

ALONG THE RIVER

The Lost River
Community Association Newsletter

Well, it's official. Spring has sprung, and as that gentleman bard Browning once said, 'Oh, to be in England now that April's there.' But with all our flowers bursting with color and splash, I say I would much rather be in Lost River. Have you ever seen a prettier spring? And of course it's getting to be that time of year when Mr. Peter Cottontail is about ready to come hopping down that bunny trail. All you boys and girls out there be

119

sure to come for the big Easter egg hunt that will be held at the community hall, and a big thanks to Mr. Oswald T. Campbell for volunteering to help dye Easter eggs this year.

— Dottie Nivens

A Visit

Miss Alma was having her nap and Oswald was out on the river, so Betty Kitchen had a moment to walk next door and have a cup of coffee with Frances. After they had finished discussing Polka Dot business, she said, 'You know, Frances, we are all going to have to be extra special nice to Mr. Campbell.'

'Why?'

'Last night I asked him if he had any family and he told me no, he was an orphan named after a can of soup. He said he did not have a living relative that he knew of.'

Frances was appalled. 'Oh, poor Mr. Campbell, and he never mentioned a word to me about it. Betty, can you think of anything worse than being an orphan?'

Betty thought it over for a moment. 'Well,' she said, 'I wouldn't mind giving it a try, for a day or so at least. Mother is about to drive me batty. I came in this morning and she had poured four boxes of oatmeal and two bottles of Log Cabin syrup all over my kitchen floor. You try cleaning that up.'

'What possessed her to do that?'

Betty shrugged. 'Who knows what possesses her to do anything? Yesterday she was hiding from Eskimos she saw flying around in the yard and locked herself in the attic. Poor Butch had to come over in the middle of the night and break the lock to get her out. She's worse than trying to keep track of a litter of kittens.'

After Betty left, Frances thought about poor Mr. Campbell. Even though she did have her sister Mildred and plenty of relatives, she knew what it felt like to be lonely. Mr. Campbell deserved to find someone, even if it was late in his life. There was always hope, and now that he had put on a little weight he was almost nice-looking. Why Mildred would waste so much time over that Billy Jenkins who had left her practically at the altar was beyond her. She knew Mr. Campbell liked Mildred. Why else would he laugh at her terrible jokes?

Just as she was finishing the dishes, she heard someone knocking at her door and wondered who it was. She dried her hands and walked to the door, and there stood Tammie Suggs and she did not look happy. Oh dear, thought Frances, I could be in trouble. She had bought Patsy a pair of gloves on the sly. But she put on her best smile and said, 'Well, hello, Mrs. Suggs, how nice to see you. Won't you come in?'

As Frances opened the door she looked out and saw a banged-up maroon truck parked in front of her house with a long-haired man sitting in the driver's seat. Tammie marched into the living room, flopped down in her best chair, and said, 'The reason I've come here is because my husband showed back up yesterday, and we're fixing to leave for Arkansas in the morning.'

Frances's heart sank. She had known this day was coming, but she had hoped to have a little more time with Patsy.

'I'm sorry to hear that, Mrs. Suggs. I'm sure we will all miss Patsy.'

'Here's the thing,' Tammie said. 'I know you took sort of an interest in her and all, and my husband said he don't want to fool with her no more, so I was wondering if you knew anybody that might be willing to have her for a while.'

Frances was totally unprepared for the question but, not missing a beat, she looked Tammie right in the eye. 'I do know somebody, Mrs. Suggs,' she said. 'Me. I would just love to have that little girl.'

Tammie said, 'Well, all right, then, you can have her this afternoon if you want.' And she gave the child away with no more concern than if she had just given away an old sweater.

After Tammie and the husband drove off, Frances was beside herself with joy. She had prayed for a child for years and every Christmas Eve had secretly longed to have a little girl of her own to send up and get a present from Santa Claus. When her husband died she had given up hope. But now her prayers had been answered. She was so grateful, she thanked the Good Lord that Tammie had come to her first and wondered why she had ever doubted Him. She ran upstairs to get the room ready for Patsy and to think about all the things she was going to buy her. She would buy her a hundred pairs of shoes, and Patsy could ruin all of them, as far as she was concerned.

Frances called everyone she knew and told them the good news. They were all delighted and relieved that Patsy was finally going to have a good home. Later that day, after Frances had the room ready, she went down to the store and explained to Patsy that she was coming home to live with her now. Patsy, who had been left in so many different places in her short life and always went where she was told to go, said OK. She told Jack goodbye and that she would see him in the morning. That first afternoon as Frances walked down the street with Patsy, holding her hand all the way back up to her house, people up and down all came out on their porches and waved at them as they passed. Dottie called out with a flourish, 'Helloo, Miss Patsy, we're all so glad you're going to stay with us!'

It soon became a familiar sight, Frances walking the little girl in the Dr Pepper hat to the store every morning and back home every afternoon.

★ ★ ★

In all the excitement of getting Patsy, it was not until a few days later that Frances realized Tammie Suggs had left without giving her a forwarding address. Not only that, she also realized she had no idea what Patsy's last name was. But it didn't really make any difference. Frances had her now, and that was all that mattered. She and Mildred took Patsy to Mobile and bought her shoes and socks, underwear, dresses, coats, and sweaters. They tried to buy her a few cute hats but Patsy did not want any hat other than the Dr Pepper beanie Mr. Campbell had given her. She wore it with everything. Even when Frances washed her hair and combed it out so nice and shiny, she put the hat right back on. On the first Sunday, when Frances dressed her up in a frilly white dress, she put the beanie on again and Frances didn't have the heart to make her take it off, so she wore it to church. She would have slept in it if Frances had let her.

As the days went by, Frances worried that Patsy might be upset at coming to live with a complete stranger, but if she missed Tammie Suggs or her father, she never said so. She never complained about anything, really. She was basically a very shy and quiet child and seemed perfectly happy to do what she was told. Although Frances did not know how old Patsy was, she guessed she must be at least six and planned on sending her to first grade in the fall. But before she went, Frances wanted to teach her a few basic things so she would have a head start. Even though December was still eight months away, she wanted to make sure that Patsy would be able to write a letter to Santa Claus next Christmas and go up and get her present from Santa with all the other children.

Every afternoon after the store closed, Patsy would come home and have her lessons. Mildred came by and asked how Patsy was doing, and Frances beamed with pride. 'Oh, Mildred, she's as bright as a penny, she can already write her name and she's reading like a house afire.' She turned and exclaimed, 'Why, she may be a genius for all we know!'

Mildred was genuinely happy for her sister, but she was also worried. 'Now, Frances, don't let yourself get too attached to this child, you're just setting yourself up to have your heart broken when that father comes back for her. It's not like you can keep her forever.'

'I know that,' said Frances. 'I know I only have her for a little while.'

'Well, just as long as you understand,' Mildred said. 'I don't want you to get too attached and forget that she belongs to someone else.' But her sister's warning was too late. Frances had already become attached. Secretly she hoped that the little girl would never have to leave.

★   ★   ★

When Oswald wasn't at the store visiting with Patsy or at the river, he worked on his sketches on the back porch of the Kitchen house. One rainy afternoon when he was on the porch, Betty walked out to get something from the extra ice box she kept out there, glanced at his latest picture, and exclaimed, 'That looks just like a blue jay!' And then she added, 'I hate blue jays,' and went back in the kitchen.

But Oswald was very encouraged. Not that Betty hated blue jays but that she had recognized what he had drawn. When he had first started, all his birds looked alike. He must be getting better.

126

Oswald was now spending most of his cigarette money on painting supplies, but that was all right with him. He was smoking less anyway.

A few days later, Oswald asked Claude Underwood, who went fishing every morning at 6 A.M., if he would take him back up in the marshes. He wanted to see the large ospreys and their nests that he had been told were there. There was a picture of them in his Alabama birds book, but so far he had not spotted any.

'Sure,' said Claude, happy to oblige. 'I can get you right up to them and leave you there for a couple of hours, if you like.' Claude had seen some of his drawings and was pleased that Oswald had found something he seemed to enjoy. He noticed that Oswald was getting a lot of mail now from the Alabama Ornithological and Audubon Society.

The next morning at five-thirty Oswald walked over to Claude's house. He saw a light on in the kitchen and knocked gently. Claude's wife, Sybil, opened the door and greeted him with a big smile. 'Come on in, Mr. Campbell, and have a cup of coffee. Claude's getting the boat ready.' He stepped into a big room, with pine walls and a brick fireplace that had a large circular brown-and-cream rug in front of it. The sofa and the easy chair and the curtains in the windows all had the same brown-checked material, and hanging over the fireplace was a picture of the Last Supper. A round honey-colored maple dining table, with a lazy Susan and chairs, was across the room. The place was neat and clean and looked as if it had not changed one bit since it was first decorated, which by the look of the pinecone wallpaper in the kitchen, Oswald guessed was probably sometime in the forties. 'A place where time itself stood still,' came to his mind as he sat down and was handed a cup of coffee and a homemade cinnamon bun by Sybil, who also looked like she was from the forties. She had on a white frilly apron over her housedress and still wore her hair in tight curls that only old-fashioned bobby pins could create. 'Claude tells me you are going across the river to look at some birds for your art.'

He laughed. 'Mrs. Underwood, I don't know if you can call it art, but yes, I'm going to try and do a few sketches.'

Sybil poured him another cup of coffee. 'I think it's very exciting,' she said. 'Claude tells me you are a wonderful artist. Who knows, Mr. Campbell, one day you may be hanging in a museum and make us all famous.'

Claude came through the front door. 'Good morning,' he said. 'We can take off anytime you're ready.'

'I'm ready,' said Oswald, picking up his sketch pad. Sybil handed each of them a small paper bag.

Mr. Campbell looked at his sack. 'What's this?'

'Your lunch,' she said. 'You don't think I'd send you boys off with nothing to eat, do you?'

It had been years since anyone had called Oswald a boy, and he liked it. As they walked to the river, he said, 'Your wife is really nice. How

128

long have you been married?'

'Forty-one years this July.'

Then Claude, who was usually a man of few words, said something surprising. 'And I don't mind telling you that there has not been a day in all those years that I haven't thanked the Good Lord for her.'

★ ★ ★

The river was still covered with early morning mist as they headed out. After about an hour, the mist lifted and the sun came up over the salty marshes that now lay before them. Claude pointed to some tall gray trees that had great nests on the tops of them. 'There they are.' As they approached the bank of the river, a big hawklike bird rose up and gently flapped to another tree, and perched there, looking at them. 'If you're lucky you'll see all kinds of owls and hawks and cranes, they live up in these marshes.' Claude pulled up alongside a dock with a wooden bench and let him out. 'I'll be back to get you in a few hours.'

As Claude pulled away and disappeared around the bend and the sound of his motor faded away Oswald realized that he was truly out in the middle of nowhere. After a while back up in the marshes with only the sound of occasional wings flapping and a hoot owl way off in the distance to break the silence, Oswald began to lose all sense of time and place. All the years of catechism, and years of drinking, had not done it, but now, sitting in the silence, away from 'the whirl of society and the noise of city life,' he felt himself becoming one with nature. For the first time in his life he was at peace. He had finally caught a glimpse of what they had been talking about.

* * *

Around ten o'clock he started to get hungry, so he opened the sack and looked in. Sybil had packed him a typical fisherman's lunch: a box of saltine crackers and small tins of potted meat, tiny Vienna sausages, and sardines. She had included a white plastic knife and several packets of mustard and he ate the whole thing and it was delicious. An hour later, Claude came to pick him up, and when he got in the boat Claude said, 'Any luck?'

'Oh, yes, I must have seen a hundred birds,' he said. 'What about you?'

'A little,' Claude said, as they headed home. Oswald found out later that for Claude a little luck meant he had caught more fish and bigger fish than anyone on the river, not just that day but also that week. There was no question that he had a talent for fishing. He knew the currents and how to read them, how the wind affected the fish, how deep they were at what time of the year. Some who had been with him said he could hear them. But he was modest, and when he was asked how he did it he just said, 'I do a lot of it and stick with it longer, I guess.' The only time he did not fish was on Saturday afternoon when everybody in Lost River had the Saturday opera

130

on the radio and you could hear it up and down the river. Claude said there was no point to try because all those Italians screaming like that scared the fish so bad they wouldn't bite anyway.

When Oswald had first been told that Claude Underwood went fishing every day of his life he could not comprehend how anybody could be so obsessed with one thing. But since he had started painting he understood completely. Still, he had a different reason to paint every day for as long as he possibly could. He wanted to be good enough to paint that one picture he had in mind and he hoped to finish it by Christmas. So while Claude fished, Oswald painted, and the river just kept quiet and let them do it.

★ ★ ★

At the next Mystic Order of the Royal Polka Dots Secret Society meeting, the annual election of officers was held. As usual, Frances was voted back in as president, Sybil Underwood as vice president, Mildred as treasurer, and Dottie Nivens as secretary. Betty Kitchen never stood for election. Because of her height and her military background, she had been named sergeant at arms, in perpetuity.

When the election was over, Mildred complained. 'I don't know why we even bother to have the dumb thing anyway; we always elect the same old people.' And after another show of hands, a vote was taken to change the election to every other year. At the same meeting, before they concluded their business, they also voted to

131

reciprocate and invite the members of the Mystic Order of the Royal Dotted Swiss secret society over for a luncheon. Although they were a sister organization and often did projects together, there was also a small friendly rivalry between the two, and so elaborate plans were made. When they had been the Dotted Swiss's luncheon guests over at Lillian, they were served Pineapple Chicken Salad with date-nut bread and cream cheese. The Polka Dots decided that they would serve tomato aspic, three different breads, and a floating island for dessert. Nobody could top Sybil's floating island. Plus they would make table favors of polka-dotted pot holders to be at each plate. 'That ought to impress them,' declared Betty Kitchen.

A Sighting

A few weeks later, after Claude had dropped him off way up in the marshes again, Oswald had quite a start. He had been lost in his work and had not heard it coming, but when he looked up there was a boat sitting not more than five feet in front of him. The dark-skinned man in the boat was staring at him with a look that made his blood run cold. After a long moment he slowly began to paddle away, never saying a word. When Claude came back, Oswald described the man with blue-green eyes and silver hair to him and asked if he knew who he was.

Claude asked if he had a net in the back of his boat.

Oswald said he did.

Claude nodded. 'I have a pretty good idea who it was, all right.'

'Who?'

'I can't say for sure, but I think you might have just had yourself an up-close look at Julian LaPonde.'

'The Creole?'

'Sounds like him.'

'He didn't look too friendly, I can tell you that.'

'No, he wouldn't.'

'I didn't say anything.'

'It's best that you didn't. You never know which way he's liable to jump.'

'What should I do if he comes back?'

'He won't . . . believe me. He doesn't want a thing to do with any of us. If he could pick up his side of the river and move it to Louisiana, he would.'

Claude was right. Oswald did not see him again.

* * *

As the days got warmer, Patsy would sometimes go out with Claude and Oswald to the marshes and sit with Oswald for hours while he painted. One day he looked over and said, 'Hey, Patsy, what are you going to be when you grow up, do you know yet?'

She thought about it. 'Hmmm . . . maybe a . . . I don't know.'

'Well, is there anything you like to do?'

'I like to play with Jack. I like birds.'

'Ah,' he said. 'Maybe you can be a veterinarian one day. Do you know what a veterinarian is?'

'No, sir.'

'It's a doctor who takes care of animals and birds. Would you like that?'

'Yes, I would. Could I be a real doctor?'

'Sure. If you want to bad enough you can.'

'Really? Could Jack come and see me?'

'Absolutely.'

Her eyes suddenly lit up. 'If I was a doctor, maybe I could fix his wing so he could fly so good that the hawks and owls couldn't catch him and eat him.'

'Maybe you could.' Then Oswald handed Patsy a small picture he had drawn for her of a large white crane, wearing glasses, tap shoes, and a top hat and carrying a walking stick under his wing. Underneath was written: *For Patsy, Mr. Ichabod Crane, Putting on the Ritz.*

That night when she came back home, Frances was at the sewing machine busy making borders for the pot holders and Patsy said, 'Mrs. Cleverdon, guess what I'm going to be when I grow up?'

'Oh, I just wouldn't have any idea.'

'Guess.'

'Let's see. A teacher?' said Frances.

'No.'

'A cowboy?'

'No.' She laughed. 'Do you want me to tell you?'

'Yes.'

The girl's eyes lit up. 'A bird doctor!'

'A bird doctor? Oh, my, where did you come up with that?'

'Mr. Campbell. He said if I wanted to bad enough I could. He said all you have to do is want something really, really bad, and if it's supposed to it will happen.'

'He did?'

'Yes, he said he always wanted to paint and he wished and wished really really hard, and now he's doing it!'

Patsy showed her the picture Oswald had done for her that day. 'Oh, this is very good,' Frances said. 'He's just getting better and better, isn't he? Your aunt Mildred should see this.' She gave her back the picture. 'You like Mr. Campbell, don't you?'

'Yes, ma'am, he's funny.'

After Patsy went to bed, Frances thought about what Mr. Campbell had told Patsy and realized he might be right. She must have wanted a child *really* badly because she got one. Now she found herself actually praying that Patsy's father would never come back and take her away. She knew it was wrong to pray for something like that, but she couldn't help it.

The Stranger

It was a warm humid afternoon in late May when a black car drove up in front of the store and parked. Roy was behind the counter by the cash register, laughing and telling Oswald that when he had come in that morning Jack had had his foot stuck in a flyswatter. Betty Kitchen was over in the produce department, examining the potatoes. When the man in the white shirt and dark shiny pants walked in and stood looking around the store, Roy looked up. 'Can I help you find something?'

The man wiped his brow and the back of his neck with a handkerchief and said, 'Yeah, I'll take something cold to drink if you have it. It's a hot one out there.'

Roy pointed to the drink box. 'Help yourself.'

'Thanks,' the man said.

Roy didn't know why, but he had a strange feeling about the guy, so he looked out the window and saw that his car was from Montgomery, the state capital, and it had an official state seal on the door. This guy was not lost or just stopping in for a drink. He was here on some sort of official business. While the man was looking in the box with his back turned, Roy slowly walked around and stood in front of the photograph taped against the side of the cash register.

The man came over with his drink. 'I wonder if you could help me out. I'm trying to locate a Mrs. Tammie Suggs. I understand that she and her family used to live around here.' When Betty Kitchen heard the name Suggs, she started throwing potatoes in her bag a mile a minute.

Roy leaned back up against the cash register, crossed his arms, and thought out loud. 'Hmm, Suggs . . . Suggs . . . Nope, doesn't ring a bell.'

In the meantime, Oswald had slowly floated away from the cash register back into the store and was pretending to be looking for something on the shelf.

Roy took a toothpick out of his pocket, looked at it, then put it in the corner of his mouth and calmly asked, 'Why are you trying to locate this Suggs woman. Any special reason?'

The man said, 'I'm really looking for the little girl we were told she has in her possession.' All of a sudden Jack started running around his plastic wheel and ringing his bells like crazy, as if he too understood the danger of the moment. The man continued, 'I'm looking on behalf of the father' — he took a piece of paper out of his pocket and read, 'A James Douglas Casey who left her in custody of the Suggs family. We have this area on file as their last known location.'

'Huh,' said Roy and turned around. 'Miss Kitchen, does the name Suggs ring a bell with you?'

'Never heard of them,' Betty said, as she moved on to the squash.

Roy called out to the back of the store. 'Hey, Mr. Campbell, do you know of any Suggs family that used to live around here? Had a little girl with them?'

Oswald, who had been standing frozen in one spot, staring at a can of pork and beans said, 'Suggs? No, the only family that might have been them moved to Mexico. I think they said they were going to Juárez or was it Cuernavaca? One of those places down there.'

'Mexico?' the man asked. 'Are you sure they said Mexico?'

'Yeah,' said Oswald, picking up a can of butter beans and pretending to read the label. 'They told me they weren't coming back, either, some trouble with the law or something.'

'Huh,' said the man.

About that time Claude came in the door carrying a bucket of fish and Roy immediately said, 'Oh, hello, Mr. Underwood, how are you today?' and cleared his throat. 'Maybe you can help us out. This gentleman here is looking for a girl that lived back up in the woods with a family named Suggs. Mr. Campbell remembers there was a family back there with a little girl that took off and went to Mexico, Juárez or Cuernavaca. Isn't that right, Mr. Campbell?'

'That's right,' said Oswald, who was now in the breakfast cereal section.

Claude had figured out something was wrong the minute Roy called him Mr. Underwood. He put the bucket of fish up on the counter and said, 'I hate to disagree with you, Oswald, but I heard those folks you are talking about say they were headed out to Canada.'

The man looked at him. 'Canada?'

Claude took his cap off and scratched his head. 'Yeah, as I recall it they said they were going up to Quebec.'

'Maybe you're right,' said Oswald, picking up a box of Blue Diamond stove matches. 'I knew it was somewhere that began with a Q.'

Claude said, 'No, wait a minute . . . Now that I think about it, it *could* have been Mexico. I know it was one of those places but if I were you I'd try looking in Mexico first.'

'Oh, brother.' The man sighed. 'By the time I go through all the red tape down there, the kid will be grown.'

'So,' said Roy, as casually as he could, even managing a yawn, 'the father wants the girl back?'

The man took a swig of his Coke and shook his head. 'No, not really. The father's dead. Fell off the back of a truck a couple of months ago. The grandmother claims she's too old to take care of the little girl so she signed her over to us, and now all I have to do is find her.'

'Who is us?' asked Roy.

'The State of Alabama. She's an official ward of the state now.'

At that moment, Betty Kitchen glanced out the window and saw Patsy coming down the street, headed straight for the front door. Betty immediately grabbed her sack of groceries and swept her way past the men at the cash register. 'I'll pay you tomorrow,' she said, and was out the door. With her sack in one arm, she snatched

140

Patsy up off the ground with the other and had her headed back home to Frances in less than five seconds. Betty had not been an emergency room nurse for nothing. She could move fast when she had to. The man in the store, who had missed the entire episode, continued to complain about his job. 'I waste half my life running up and down the roads trying to track these people down and — ' He stopped in mid-sentence. 'What are those bells I'm hearing?'

Roy said, 'It's just a bird I've got back there.'

'Oh,' he said.

'Say,' said Roy. 'Just out of curiosity. What will happen to her when you do find her?'

'Well,' he said, looking around at all the mounted fish and animals on the wall, 'being she has no other living relatives, she'll most likely be sent to a state home until she's eighteen.'

Oswald flinched when he heard that. Just the thought of Patsy being raised in a state home almost made him sick to his stomach. The man walked over, looked into the bucket, and said, 'Nice fish.' Then he put his empty bottle on the counter and sighed again. 'Well, thanks for your help, but from what you fellows tell me it doesn't look likely that I will find that little girl anytime soon. You try tracking somebody down in Mexico or in Canada.' He then asked Roy what he owed for the Coke.

'Nothing.' said Roy. 'I'm always happy to accommodate a government man.'

'Much obliged,' he said, and handed Roy his card. 'My name is Brent Boone: that's my

141

numbers on the bottom. Call me if you hear anything.'

Roy said, 'Yeah, we sure will, Mr. Boone.'

Boone went to the door muttering to himself. 'Mexico, of all the damn places.' Then he turned around at the door and said, 'Well, wish me luck, fellows. God knows I'll need it.'

'Yeah,' said Roy. 'Good luck.' And they all watched him drive away. Roy picked up the phone to call Frances. As far as they were concerned, from that day on Patsy was officially theirs, and Oswald walked home that night grinning from ear to ear. Patsy Casey was her name. She was Irish, just like him!

The Assistant

As the summer progressed, it seemed everything was looking up. Oswald continued to feel well, and the Dotted Swiss luncheon was a huge success. The Dotted Swiss ladies, who tended to lord it over the Polka Dots as far as their needlework was concerned, had been very impressed with the pot holders, and Frances could tell they were green with envy over the tomato aspic. Not only had the luncheon been a hit, Patsy was very happy. She had a brand-new job.

★   ★   ★

In the past, when asked, Roy had taken Jack out and done a few little shows with him for local schools or church bazaars to raise money. But the next time he and Jack were asked to do a show, Roy asked Frances if Patsy could come along. She said yes, she thought it was a fine idea. After that, whenever he and Jack did a show, he started taking Patsy along as his assistant. Frances even bought her a special red-striped dress to wear to match Roy's red-and-white-striped jacket and straw hat. Oswald went with them and helped set up chairs for the performance. Roy would start the show with Patsy standing beside him and Jack perched on his finger.

'Come one, come all, come and see the Amazing Redbird of Baldwin County. He walks, he talks, he crawls on his belly like a snake. The only redbird in captivity that actually knows his own name! And now, my lovely assistant Miss Patsy and I will demonstrate. Is your name Jack?' The bird would bob up and down as if he were agreeing. 'Yes! he says. Absolutely amazing. But wait. Now you might think a poor dumb bird would not know his right from his left. But observe the Amazing Redbird of Baldwin County.' At this point Patsy would hold out her right finger and Jack would land on it. 'That is correct, sir! And now the left.' Jack would fly over to her left hand. 'Absolutely amazing! The only redbird in America, ladies and gentlemen, boys and girls of all ages, that can tell me exactly what I have hidden here in my hand.' Then the bird would walk up her arm to her shoulder and nudge her ear. 'And what did he say the object was, Miss Patsy?' He would lean down while Patsy whispered something to him. 'The bird has said, *Sunflower seeds.*'

Roy then opened his hand to reveal about ten shiny black sunflower seeds. 'He is absolutely correct yet again! Ladies and gentlemen! I can hardly believe it myself.' Then Patsy would pretend the bird said something else in her ear and tug on Roy's jacket and Roy would hold up his hand and say, 'Wait a moment, ladies and gentlemen, the bird has spoken again.' Then

Patsy would whisper again to Roy. 'Ah-ha!' said Roy. 'The Amazing Redbird of Baldwin County says he would like to demonstrate his powers of detection. Very well. At this time I will hide certain objects and test his abilities. Please turn your back, Miss Patsy, while I hide the objects.' Patsy would turn away with Jack, as Roy would make a big show out of hiding seeds in all his pockets; later of course Jack, who was a glutton for sunflower seeds, amazed the audience as he crawled in and out of all Roy's pockets and found every one.

After the shows children would come up and try to talk to Patsy, but Roy noticed that she seemed shy and afraid of other children.

Frances saw it too, and it worried her. She tried to invite a few children over to the house to play with Patsy, but it was no good. All Patsy wanted to do was play with Jack. Frances wondered if, in the past, children had been mean to her because of her leg. The first time she had bathed her she had been surprised to see how badly twisted her little body was. She just hoped, when Patsy went to school in the fall, that the other children would not make fun of her.

Two Men in a Boat

Claude heard the redfish were biting and had gone all the way up the river over to Perdido Bay. As he was coming home up the backside of the river late that afternoon, he heard somebody yelling, 'Help! Help! Help!'

He saw two men standing up in a shiny brand-new blue-and-white twenty-two-foot boat in the middle of the river, frantically waving.

He throttled down his motor and pulled up alongside them. 'Hey, fellows, what's up?'

'Thank God you came along! We've been stranded out here all day,' one man said.

The other man said, 'We must have hit something, because the motor just died and wouldn't start again and we've been drifting around for hours. We must have drifted five miles.'

Claude asked, 'Why didn't you use your paddles?'

'They didn't give us any,' the man said.

Claude calmly pointed over at the right side of the boat. 'Look in that compartment down there. There should be a couple.'

The larger man opened the long side panel and saw two paddles. 'Oh.'

'Where did you fellows come from?'

'We started out at the Grand Hotel at Point Clear. Where are we now?'

'You're all the way to Lost River, about fifteen miles south.'

'How are we going to get all the way back?'

'Well, let me take a look at this thing.' Claude maneuvered around the back of the boat and quickly assessed the situation. 'You got your motor all twisted up with silt and mud.'

'Can it be fixed?'

'Oh, sure, but we've got to pull it out of the water to do it.' He threw them a rope and towed them back to his house. When they pulled up to the dock, Claude looked at the setting sun and said, 'It'll be too dark to get you to the hotel by boat tonight, but I'll get Butch to drive you back and the hotel can send somebody to get your boat tomorrow.'

As the two men gathered up their expensive fishing gear and heavy rods and reels, Claude chuckled. 'What were you boys aiming to catch out there today?'

Embarrassed that they had to be towed in, they tried to sound like they knew what they were doing. 'Oh, speckled trout, redfish. I hear they're running pretty good this time of year.'

'Uh-huh,' said Claude. 'About the only thing you're liable to catch with that stuff you got there is a shark — or a whale, maybe.'

He opened a box and pulled out a string of the biggest bass, redfish, and speckled trout they had ever seen.

'Come on up to the house and I'll call Butch.'

'Thanks, that's mighty nice of you.'

'By the way,' said the larger one, 'my name is Tom and this is Richard.'

'I'm Claude Underwood. Nice to meet you.'

As the three of them headed up the yard, Claude said, 'You boys down here on a vacation?'

'No,' said Tom, 'we're attending a medical convention at the hotel, but we thought we might try to get a little fishing in while we're here.'

When they got to the house Sybil fixed them some coffee and a few minutes later Butch came in the door whistling. He was used to being called to take amateur fishermen back home. It gave him a chance to have some fun. 'Hey, guys, I hear you got lost. That's why we call it Lost River, 'cause if you're up this far, you must be lost.' And as always he laughed at his own joke, thinking it was the funniest thing he had ever heard.

When they were leaving, Claude said, 'How long are you here for?'

Tom said, 'Just three more days. Unfortunately this one was shot to hell.' He looked over at Sybil. 'Excuse me, ma'am.'

Sybil laughed. 'Don't worry, I'm married to a fisherman so I've heard that kind of language before.'

Claude, who felt sorry for them, said, 'If you want to do some more fishing, come back tomorrow and I'll take you out and show you a few good spots.'

Later, when Butch was driving them back to the hotel, he said, 'You might not know it, but you just met the best fisherman in the state. If he's offered to take you out, you need to take him up on it.'

'Thanks! We will,' they said.

*　*　*

The next afternoon Butch picked them up and drove them back down to the river to where Claude was waiting for them at the dock.

'Hey, boys, get in,' he said. They climbed into his old green fourteen-foot flat-bottom boat powered by a small five-horse Johnson motor and headed out. Claude handed them both a simple rod and reel and explained his method. 'I only use this little guy here.' He held up a red and white Heddon vamp spook. 'Now I modify it a bit, I take the front lip off and it runs deeper for you. Or else I just use a little lead head jig, but that's all you really need.'

Before the day was over, the two men were so excited they could hardly believe it. They had caught more fish and learned more about fishing in one day than they had all their lives. They thought Claude must have some sort of secret knowledge about fish. Claude, always philosophical, said, 'Naw, there's no secret to it. Either they're biting or they ain't.'

*　*　*

The men came down the next two afternoons and had a wonderful time going up and down the river with Claude, and he got a kick out of the two who were obviously city boys, full of

149

enthusiasm and excitement every time they caught something. On the last day they were to be there, they tried to pay him for being their guide, but Claude said, 'No. You don't owe me a thing.'

Tom said, 'We'd love to pay you for your time.'

'Thank you, but no, it was my pleasure.'

'Are you sure?'

'Yes, I'm sure. You fellows don't owe me a dime. But I am going to ask you to do me a favor.'

'If we can, sure, what is it?'

'I know you fellows are both doctors, and I wondered if you would take a look at a little girl for me and tell me what you think.'

★　★　★

In the past few days Claude had found out that the two men were at the hotel for the southeastern convention of elbow and shoulder surgeons. He did not know if they could help Patsy but he thought it might be worth a try, so he told Frances to have Patsy up at his house that afternoon just in case they agreed to see her.

Frances dressed Patsy in her best dress and brought her over, and they sat in the living room with Sybil and Butch and waited for them. When the two men walked in with Claude, he introduced them to Frances and then to Patsy. Tom leaned down and shook her hand. 'Hi, Patsy, how are you?' Then he said, 'Honey, could you do me a big favor? Would you walk across the room for me?' Patsy looked at Frances, who

150

smiled and motioned for her to do it. Patsy walked across the room and stopped. Tom whispered something to his friend and said, 'Now come on back for me.' She did. 'That's fine, thank you, honey,' he said. After a few more minutes of small talk, they said their goodbyes and walked out the door.

Claude and Butch followed them out, and they stood in the yard and talked. Tom said, 'Mr. Underwood, unfortunately that sort of birth injury is not our specialty. We deal mostly with sports injuries. I wish we could help, but that girl needs a specialist.'

'What kind of specialist?'

'She needs a pediatric orthopedic surgeon,' said Richard. 'Kids' bones are tricky, and you need someone with a lot of skill and expertise in that area.'

Tom looked at his friend and said a name: 'Sam Glickman.'

Richard nodded. 'Yeah.'

★ ★ ★

Later that night the phone rang. 'Mr. Underwood, this is Tom. Listen. If you can get that little girl up here to the hotel before eight o'clock in the morning, Sam says he will take a quick look at her before he has to catch his plane back to Atlanta.'

Claude called Frances and told her to have Patsy ready and that Butch would pick them up at six-thirty and drive them over to the hotel. When Frances told Patsy that they were going

151

for a ride in the morning, she asked if Mr. Campbell could go with them.

'Well, if you want him to, I'll call and see.'

When she phoned and asked, Oswald said, 'If Patsy wants me to come, I'll be there.'

When he hung up he was so pleased that Patsy had wanted him to go along, he felt like a million bucks. Would he go? Why, he would have gone to the moon and back if she had asked.

★ ★ ★

The next morning Butch drove the three of them all the way over to Point Clear, to the Grand Hotel on the Mobile Bay. At seven-thirty, wearing only her underwear and her Dr Pepper hat, Patsy was lying on a banquet table in the main dining room being examined by Dr. Samuel Glickman. Frances and Oswald both cringed as they watched the doctor push and pull her leg back and forth, up and down. Then he turned her over and felt all the way up her spine, talking to her the whole time he was examining her. 'You know, Patsy,' he said, 'I have a little granddaughter about your age named Colbi, and do you know what she told me? Does that hurt?' Patsy made a face like it did but said, 'No, sir.' Then he turned her back over. 'She said, 'Granddaddy, I already have two boy-friends.' Can you imagine that?' As he sat her up and had her bend over to the left as far as she could and then to the right, he asked, 'Do you have a boyfriend?'

'No, sir,' she said.

152

'Yes, you do, Patsy,' Frances said. 'You told me the other day that Jack was your boyfriend. Tell the doctor about Jack, honey.'

* * *

After it was all over, the doctor looked at his watch, picked up his suitcase, and said to Frances, 'Come walk to the car with me, Mrs. Cleverdon.' Then he turned and smiled and waved. 'Goodbye, Patsy.'

He talked as they walked through the lobby.

'Mrs. Cleverdon, I would need to do X-rays, of course, but from what I felt I would say that her pelvis and right hip were broken in four, maybe five places, and whoever did it never bothered to set the bones straight. Does she complain much about pain?'

Frances, running to keep up with him, said, 'No, Doctor, she's never said a word about pain.'

'Well, I don't know why she hasn't, because I know it has to hurt. Those bones are pressing on the nerves in her hip and spine, and the more she grows the worse it will get.'

As he got in the waiting car, Frances blurted out the one question they all wanted answered. 'Can anything be done?'

Dr. Glickman looked up. 'Mrs. Cleverdon, it's not a question of can anything be done. Something has to be done.' He handed her a card. 'Call my office and set up an appointment,' he said, and the car drove away.

Frances went back inside and found them all

153

waiting in the lobby for her. 'He wants to see her in his office,' she said.

* ★ *

Two weeks later they were swerving in and out of Atlanta traffic while Frances and Oswald reached back and forth over Patsy trying to read the map. Finally, they found the medical building and made it on time.

Frances said, 'How anybody can find their way in or out of this town is a mystery to me.'

After a series of X-rays were looked at and all the tests were done, Dr. Glickman called Frances and Oswald into his office while a nurse took Patsy down to the cafeteria for something to eat.

'With a malformation as severe as this,' he said, 'if we let it go uncorrected any longer, what will happen is that she will begin to lose mobility and eventually she won't be able to walk at all.'

Frances grabbed Oswald's hand for support. 'Oh, dear.'

'And as she continues to grow it will begin to affect her central nervous system as well. The sooner we can reset those bones and relieve her skeletal and muscular area from all the stress and strain the better. But we are talking about two — maybe three — separate surgeries. With a child that young and frail it's a pretty serious undertaking, and it's going to require a lot of strength and stamina on her part to get through it.'

Frances was alarmed. 'You don't mean she could die, do you?'

154

'With any major surgery there's always that possibility, of course, but from what I have seen she seems like a pretty happy little girl with a lot to live for. But let me be clear. She will need a lot of emotional support from all of us for the long haul, and even after going through it all there are still no guarantees she will heal properly.'

'Oh, dear,' said Frances again.

'Having said all that, in my opinion it has to be done. I just want you to know up front that it is going to be a long hard process, no matter what the results.'

Oswald asked, 'Will it be expensive?'

'I wish I could say no, Mr. Campbell, but yes. It will be terribly expensive.' He glanced down at the picture of his granddaughter on his desk. And then he flipped through his calendar and looked over his glasses. 'I'll tell you what I'll do. I'll waive my surgical fees. That ought to help some. If you promise to have her here with a few more pounds on her by the end of July, we can do her first operation the morning of August second.'

Frances told the doctor that they would be there and that Patsy would have more pounds on her if she had to feed her twenty times a day. How they would get the rest of the money was another question, but she did not tell him that.

★   ★   ★

For the next month everybody up and down the street plied Patsy with cookies and candies and as much ice cream as she could eat. They were

155

determined to get those extra pounds on her by the end of July. But the main problem was going to be the money. Even without the doctor's fees it was estimated that the long hospital stay plus the following months of therapy would run over a hundred thousand dollars. Frances and Mildred had a little saved, but it was not nearly enough. The Lost River Community Association had several fund-raisers, and a large jar that said THE PATSY FUND sat by the cash register in the grocery store. Pretty soon, as more people found out about it, other organizations began to help them as well. When Elizabeth, their friend over in Lillian who was president of their sister group, the Mystic Order of the Royal Dotted Swiss, heard about it, her group held a bake and rummage sale. Lost River had a huge fish fry at the community hall every Saturday, thanks to Claude Underwood, and people came from all over the county for that. As word spread, and courtesy of Butch's friends, the Elks Club over in Elberta decided to have a fund-raiser. They planned a barbecue, and everybody in Lost River attended, along with hundreds of other people from all over the county. When Oswald got there he was in for a surprise. The members of the Alabama Accordion Association had donated their services and were giving a free concert in the park to raise money. They were up on the bandstand, dressed in lederhosen. Mr. Krause spotted Oswald and waved while playing 'The Beer Barrel Polka.' Frances and Mildred and Patsy joined him, and they sat in the wooden chairs and listened along with the rest of the people. Patsy was on her second cotton candy when suddenly Oswald saw something that made his blood run cold. He had just spotted Brent Boone, the government man, sitting in the front row across from them, and he was looking right at Patsy.

Oswald felt his ears turn red. After a few minutes Boone stood up and walked over to the large wooden barrel that had THE PATSY FUND written across it, threw in ten dollars, and headed up the aisle right toward him. As he walked past Oswald, who had stopped breathing, he looked down at him and said out of the side of his mouth, 'Mexico, my ass,' and kept going.

★   ★   ★

As August approached, Oswald wanted to do something for Patsy, but of course he had no money. But there was one thing he could try. Even if he only got a few dollars it might help.

Butch drove him over to the big Grand Hotel on the Bay in Point Clear. The last time they had been there with Patsy, he had noticed an art gallery in the lobby. Today he mustered up all his courage, walked in, and a nice lady looked at his watercolors, one at a time, but did not offer an opinion.

When she finished, she asked, 'How much are you asking for these, Mr. Campbell?' He was thrown completely; he had never sold anything in his life, much less his own work, so he said, 'Why don't you name a price?'

She looked at them again and counted. 'You

have eighteen paintings here, is that right?'

'Yes.'

She looked again and then said, 'I can offer you two hundred and fifty dollars.'

'You're kidding,' he said, thrilled beyond belief that she was willing to buy them for so much money.

'I wish I could offer you more, Mr. Campbell, these are just excellent, but we're just a small shop.'

'No, that's fine. I'll take it.'

When she handed him the check, she said, 'I'd be interested in seeing anything else you have, Mr. Campbell.'

When he got outside and looked at the check, he almost fainted.

She had meant $250.00 dollars apiece!

★ ★ ★

By the end of July, almost all the money they needed had been raised and everyone was pretty optimistic that the rest would be there on time. The morning before Patsy was to go to Atlanta for her operation, Oswald and Roy had planned to have a little going-away party for her up at the store. Roy came in around 6:45 A.M. to get ready to open and whistled for Jack. 'Hey, buddy, your girlfriend is coming to see you.' No answer. 'What have you gotten yourself into today, you nutty bird? You better not be in the marshmallows again; I don't have time to give you another bath.' He wandered around whistling and looking for the bird, and when he walked toward the front of the store he saw Jack over in the corner on the floor by the produce, his favorite place to scavenge. 'What do you have down there? You better not be pecking the tomatoes again. Mildred will be after you for sure.' He went over and looked; Jack was lying on his side. 'What are you doing, you silly thing?' When he picked him up, Jack's body felt stiff, and his usually bright eyes were strangely dull and glassed over. He looked at the bird again. Then it suddenly hit Roy like a ton of bricks. Jack was dead.

Roy stood there in shock. He could not believe that this cold lifeless thing he held in his hand was really Jack. At that moment it seemed the whole world went silent and all Roy could hear was the sound of his own heart beating. He continued to stand there stunned and not moving until after a while he finally heard Oswald knocking loudly on the front window. He looked up and Oswald waved at him. Roy went over and opened the door. Oswald could see that Roy was white as a sheet. Something was wrong.

Roy said, 'Come back to the office.'

Oswald followed him back. 'What's the matter, Roy?'

Roy closed the door and held him out. 'Jack's dead.'

'Oh, my God,' said Oswald. 'What happened?'

Roy sat down at his desk and shook his head. 'I don't know. I just found him this very minute.' Roy picked up the phone and called his veterinarian friend, who told him to look and see if Jack seemed hurt in any way. Roy looked him over. 'No, he looks fine, there's no blood or anything unusual anywhere.'

'Well, I don't know what to tell you, Roy, he could have eaten something, or caught some virus; it could have been one of a hundred things. But these things can happen very fast with birds. One day they're OK and the next day they're gone. I sure am sorry.'

Roy hung up and looked at Oswald. 'He doesn't know.'

The two men just sat there, not knowing what to say, when Oswald suddenly thought of something.

'Hey Roy,' he said. 'What about Patsy? What are we going to tell Patsy?'

Roy looked up. 'Oh, God, I didn't think about that. Get Frances on the phone and tell her not to let Patsy come up here until we figure out what to do. I'm going to put the CLOSED sign on the door.'

Oswald dialed Frances while Roy closed the blinds and turned out the lights. Frances picked up the phone.

'Hello?'

Oswald said, 'Frances, it's Oswald. I'm at the store. Where's Patsy?'

'She's right here, Mr. Campbell, just finishing her breakfast, why?'

'Thank goodness she's still there. Whatever you do, don't let her come up to the store today.'

'Oh?' she said, looking over at Patsy and not quite understanding. 'Well, that's going to be mighty hard.'

'I know it is but you have to do it. I'll explain

160

later. You just keep her there.'

Frances could tell by the tone in Mr. Campbell's voice that whatever was going on must be pretty serious. Patsy was just standing up to leave, and Frances blurted out, 'Oh, honey, I can't let you go up to the store today.'

Patsy's eyes got big. 'Why?'

'Oh, the most awful thing has happened.'

'What?'

She looked at the little girl who stood waiting for an answer. 'Poor Roy has the measles!' she said, thankful that something came to her at the very last second.

Patsy suddenly looked frightened. 'Oh, no! Does Jack have the measles too?'

'No, darling, birds don't get measles, only people.'

Frances could not imagine what had really happened. Both of them knew Patsy was leaving for the hospital tomorrow and not seeing Jack before she left would upset her terribly. The only thing she could imagine serious enough was that maybe that crazy Julian LaPonde had finally come across the river and gone on a shooting spree and shot Roy.

In a few minutes Oswald came into the backyard and caught Frances's eye from the kitchen window. He motioned for her to come over to his house.

Frances dried her hands. 'Honey, I have to run over to Betty's but I'll be right back. Now promise me you will not move from this house, OK?' She handed Patsy a coloring book and went next door. Betty and Oswald were in the living room, huddled together in hushed

161

conversation. 'What in the world is going on?' she asked.

Betty said, 'Sit down, Frances, we have terrible news.'

Frances put her hand over her mouth, 'Oh, no, it's Roy, isn't it? He's been shot, hasn't he? Is he dead?'

Betty said, 'No, it's not Roy, it's Jack. Roy came in this morning and found him.'

'Oh, my God, what happened?'

'We don't know, but that's why we didn't want Patsy coming down to the store,' Oswald said.

Frances sat down, 'Oh, dear God in heaven, what in the world are we going to tell her? You know how she feels about that bird.'

Oswald said, 'Yes, I do. How did you keep her home today?'

'I told her Roy had the measles, I didn't know what to say; I wasn't thinking straight. I also promised her she could go up to the store and say goodbye to Jack tomorrow. I didn't know he was *dead*.'

Just then Mildred came barging in the front door. 'What's going on? I went down to the store and it was closed.'

Betty shut the door behind her. 'Jack is dead.'

Mildred gasped and looked at her sister.

Frances said, 'It's true. Roy came in this morning and found him on the floor.'

'Oh, no,' cried Mildred, and then proceeded to collapse on the couch in a heap, wailing 'Oh, no! Oh, poor little Jack . . . Oh, that poor little bird. Oh, I just feel so terrible! Oh, the poor little thing.'

162

Frances looked at her like she had lost her mind. 'Mildred, what is the matter with you? Why are you suddenly carrying on like that? You did nothing but complain about him when he was alive.'

'I know I did,' Mildred wailed, 'but I always liked him. It never occurred to me he would die! Oh, poor little Jack.' She then grabbed a lace doily from the back of Betty's couch and used it as a handkerchief, which Betty did not appreciate.

'Mildred,' said Frances, 'you are, without a doubt, the strangest woman I ever knew. All you ever did was to threaten to cook him.'

'Oh, I know I did!' Mildred wailed even louder, and threw herself back down on the couch again.

Frances said, 'Oh, for God's sake, Mildred, pull yourself together,' and turned to Betty and Oswald in amazement. 'The very time I need her is the very time she decides to fall apart.'

★　★　★

Later that afternoon, while Patsy was having her nap, Butch, Betty, Dottie, Frances, and Oswald gathered in Roy's office, trying to figure out what to do. Frances explained the problem. 'The doctor told us that the operations are going to be very difficult and dangerous and right now, that bird is the one thing in this world she cares the most about. Jack is her best friend. How do you tell a child who's getting ready to go through major surgery that her best friend is dead?'

Oswald agreed with Frances. 'I don't see how we *can* tell her. I think we have to figure out what is more important here, telling the truth or taking a chance on her not making it through the operation.'

Dottie said, 'But we can't lie to her, can we? That would be wrong, wouldn't it?' She looked around the room. 'We can't lie to a child, can we?'

Betty said, 'Why not, Dottie? You do it every year at Christmas. What's the difference? Speaking as an ex-nurse with some psychological training, I say just go on to Atlanta as if nothing happened. Then later after her operations and her therapy is over, when she's healthy and out of the woods, then we tell her.'

'Yeah, Frances,' said Butch. 'Just don't tell her now.'

Frances shook her head. 'That sounds easy and I agree with you, but the problem is that I know she will not want to leave here in the morning until she tells Jack goodbye. It was all I could do to keep her at home today.'

Dottie thought for a moment. 'Could we get another redbird by morning? They all look pretty much alike, don't they? I couldn't tell one from another myself.'

Betty looked at Dottie as if she were insane and asked, 'How are we going to catch another redbird by morning? Besides, she'll know that's not the same bird. Do you think a strange bird is going to sit on her finger and do tricks?'

'Well, you think of something then,' said Dottie.

After everybody left, Roy sat holding Jack in his hand. He had been the one to realize that the only person who could help them was the one man in this world he hated. The one man he had vowed never to forgive. But there was no other way. After trying their best to think of something else, they all came to agree that this was the only solution. Poor skinny, brave Butch offered to go, and so did Betty Kitchen, but since neither of them were familiar with the other side of the river, it was decided that Roy had to go, and he had to go alone. It was the hardest thing he would ever have to do in his life: swallow every ounce of pride he had. But he made the decision to do it anyway. He had to forget about the past just this once. This was for Patsy.

He wrapped Jack in a handkerchief and placed him in his jacket pocket. Just as the sun was starting to get low in the sky, he rowed across the river to a place where he had spent most of his childhood playing on the river with the Creole families and children he had grown up with, eating gumbo and jambalaya at their mothers' tables. The happy, sunlit place he had once loved was now nothing but a shadowy murky swamp full of painful memories.

Around dusk, he pulled his boat up to the dock, walked to the long gray wooden Creole cottage where Julian LaPonde lived, and knocked on the door. No answer.

After a while he called out, 'Julian, it's Roy. I need to talk to you.' Still no answer, but someone was moving around inside. A few seconds later, when he heard the unmistakable sound of a gun click, he knew it was Julian on the other side of the screen door.

Roy was suddenly overwhelmed with old feelings of rage and humiliation. Rage at the fact that this man had ruined his life, humiliated that he had to ask for a favor instead of doing what he wanted to do — reach through the door, pull Julian out into the yard, and stomp him to death. As he continued knocking, he was even further humiliated because, for some inexplicable reason beyond his control he began to cry. He stood there with tears running down his face, as he tried to talk and hold back the sobs at the same time.

'Julian, I know you hate my guts and I hate you . . . but I want you to look at a picture of this little girl.' He took out the photograph of Patsy and Jack and held it up against the screen so he could see. 'She's a little crippled girl, Julian, and she's going off to have a really bad operation tomorrow, and the bird who was her friend died last night. If she finds out, I don't think she can make it. So I need your help.' Then he broke down completely and stood sobbing on the porch like a ten-year-old.

Julian, who had the gun aimed right at his chest and was fully prepared to shoot, hesitated for a moment. He must have seen the boy in Roy he had once known so well. After another moment he slowly put the gun down at his side and walked up closer to the door, looked at the picture, and then said to Roy in his thick Creole accent, 'I tell you . . . I kill you dead if you ever was to come over here.'

'I know.' Roy sighed. 'You can kill me later if you want to, I don't care anymore, but tonight you have to help me. I'll pay you whatever you want.'

Julian stood staring at him but made no move. He could see that in the years that had passed Roy had grown into quite a man. The only thing Roy noticed in the dim light was that Julian's thick black curly hair had turned silver. As they stood there, with Roy still pressing the picture of Patsy and Jack against the screen, Roy heard a woman's voice from inside the cottage say 'Let him in.'

After another moment, Julian growled. 'Well . . . I do it for the little gull, not you, you understand?' Roy nodded. 'Come on then,' Julian said roughly.

As Roy stepped in the room, someone said, 'Hello, Roy,' and as his eyes adjusted to the light he saw the woman, looking more beautiful than she had the last time he had seen her years ago. It was Marie.

Time had not changed the way he felt about her, and from the look in Marie's eyes, it seemed she felt the same.

★　★　★

As the sun was coming up Julian came in the kitchen and handed Jack's body back to Roy. He had worked all night and done a skillful job. All of Jack's feathers had been carefully cleaned and

167

fluffed up, and his eyes were bright and shiny. Somehow Julian had managed to take the poor dead bird he had been handed the night before and make it look alive again. Even the way the head was cocked to one side and the expression was Jack's. Roy looked at Julian and shook his head. 'It's better than I could have hoped for. I don't know what to say, Julian, except thank you.' Roy stood up and reached for his wallet in his back pocket. 'How much do I owe you?'

Julian's eyes flashed with anger. 'I tell you, I do it for the little gull. Now go.' Roy looked at Marie and nodded good-bye and then rowed back across the river with his friend.

What Roy didn't know was that the Creoles already knew about the little crippled girl named Patsy and the redbird who lived on the other side of the river. Their parish priest had been in the audience at one of the shows with Jack that he and Patsy had done for the Catholic Church over in Lillian. When he had talked about it in his sermon the following Sunday, all the Creole children who were not allowed to go across the river longed to see the redbird and the girl. And later, when the priest heard about the Patsy Fund, he had taken up a collection for her in church and sent it over as an anonymous gift. Julian, who had grown even more cold-hearted over the years and hated everybody on the other side, had not donated a dime to the fund and resented those who did. Why should they care about those people? He wouldn't lift a finger

168

to help any of them. But last night, seeing Patsy's face in the photograph smiling at him through the screen door, something happened that made him change his mind. He really had done it for the little girl.

Leaving Home

The next morning, from the moment Patsy awakened all she did was ask when she could see Jack. Frances didn't know what to tell her until she heard from Roy. Roy had gotten back to the store at around eight and Oswald was there waiting for him with his painting kit. It was around eight-thirty when Oswald finished painting red spots all over Roy's face to back up the measles story. Roy finally called a nervous Frances. When the phone rang she picked it up on the first ring.

'Hello?'

'It's me,' said Roy. Frances, pretending the call was from a boyfriend she had dated thirty-seven years ago who had been dead for six years, said, 'Oh, hello, Herbert, what a surprise to hear from you after all these years!' She was not sure if Patsy could hear her conversation but she did not want to take any chances. 'Well. So everything is OK with you?'

Roy had no idea who Herbert was and said, 'Yes, we're ready to go here. Come on anytime. Drive her up to the window, keep the motor running, slow down and stop for just a few seconds, then take off.'

'Oh, dear,' said Frances, in a high-pitched

voice. 'That will be mighty hard to do.'

'I know, but I think a few seconds is all we can chance it. Jack looks good, but if she gets too long a look she's liable to figure it out.'

'I understand completely. I'll try my very best,' she said, to the imaginary man. 'And Herbert, I'm so glad you are feeling better. Well, goodbye, and thanks for calling.'

The second she put the phone down, it rang again and she almost jumped out of her skin.

'Hello!' It was Mildred. 'Did you get the message? Roy said to drive by but don't stop for long.'

'Yes, I got the message,' she said. 'Don't be calling me now, Mildred. I've got to go!'

Frances was so nervous about the upcoming surgery, and now the bird situation, that she went to the bathroom and nearly plucked every one of her eyebrows out. She had to quickly pencil them back in with a black eyebrow pencil, but when she did they were shaped like upside down half moons. When she saw what she had done, she muttered to herself, 'Dear God, I look like a cartoon, but that just can't be helped. I'm late as it is.' She powdered her nose and fluffed her hair a few times and called out, 'Patsy, honey, it's time to go.' She put Patsy in the backseat of the car with a pillow so she could lie down along the way. Patsy looked worried and asked again, 'Can we go by and see Jack now?' Frances pretended not to hear her and reached in and honked her horn for Oswald. He walked over and put his suitcase in the trunk and got in the car. 'Good morning, Patsy,' he said, trying to

171

sound casual, but Frances could tell he was as anxious as she was. When Frances came around the other side of the car and got in, she said, 'I hope I have everything, I can't trust myself to remember anything. If I've left something, so be it. We have to leave right now or we will never get there on time.' She looked down and checked the gas. 'Good, we have a full tank.' Butch had filled it for her last night and thank goodness, because with everything that was going on she would have forgotten to do it. 'Well,' she said, 'for better or worse, here we go.'

As she pulled out of the driveway a worried Patsy said, 'Can't I go and say goodbye to Jack?'

Frances looked at her in the rearview mirror and said, 'Oh, for heaven's sake. In all this rush I almost forgot you wanted to go by and see Jack, didn't you?'

'Yes, ma'am.'

'Well, all right, I'll whip you by there, but for just a second.'

Oswald sat completely still, afraid to move a muscle, but he could not help but be impressed by the way Frances managed the sharp turn perfectly and pulled up on the other side of the gas tanks not more than fifteen feet from the front window, and stopped the car on a dime. Roy stood waiting with Jack perched upon his finger, looking as bright and alive as he ever had.

'Can't I go in?' asked Patsy.

'Oh, no, honey. Roy still has the measles. Look at him! You can't get near him. Not with you just about to be operated on. Just wave, honey,' she said as she stepped on the gas and took off. Patsy turned around and waved at Jack bobbing up and down on Roy's finger until the store and the little redbird were out of sight. As they turned onto the highway, safely headed to Atlanta, Frances was happy she had worn her dress shields. At one point after they drove off she half expected Patsy to say something, but at the moment she seemed content to at least have seen Jack, even if it had only been for a moment.

After they had been on the road awhile, Patsy took out her birthday picture with Jack and whispered to it, 'I'll be back . . . you be good now.'

The Big City

When they arrived in Atlanta and checked Patsy into the hospital, Oswald went to a pay phone. He called Roy and told him that Patsy had been fooled completely and had talked to the picture of Jack all the way. 'Honest to God, Roy,' he said, 'I know Jack is dead and it even fooled me, when you were standing there. I half expected him to fly!'

It was true. Julian had done an incredible job that night and Jack had never looked better. Roy picked him up and said, 'You pulled off your best trick ever this morning, buddy, and you didn't even know it.'

After the phone call, he carefully wrapped Jack in a soft white cloth and placed him inside something he knew Jack would appreciate being buried in. It was to be their last little joke together. Then Roy walked him way back up in the woods and dug a grave and placed the bird in the ground and covered him up. As he stood at the spot, looking down where his friend now slept in a Cracker Jack box, an old song his father used to sing ran through his head.

Nights are long, since you went away,
I think about you all through the day,
My buddy, my buddy, your buddy misses you.

Roy wondered why a six-foot-two man would cry over something no bigger than a pinecone. Damn you, Jack, he thought to himself as he walked back through the woods, if you were here I'd ring your scrawny little neck.

Roy was not a religious man, but that day he hoped if there was such a thing as a spirit, a small part of Jack's had somehow managed to escape and maybe he was up there right now, flying around looking down and laughing at all the poor earthbound creatures below. That would be just like him, Roy thought, and looked up half expecting to see him.

★   ★   ★

Frances and Oswald met at the hospital at six the next morning and sat with Patsy as nurses came in and out of the room preparing for the first operation. Oswald was busy drawing pictures for her, trying to distract her and make her laugh, while Frances tried to explain what was going to happen next. Patsy sat up in bed, wearing a hospital gown and her beanie, and seemed to be a little frightened by all the activity, but soon another nurse came in and gave her a shot to relax her and she started to get sleepy. Dr. Glickman opened the door. 'Well, good morning, young lady,' he said, as he walked over to the bed. 'How are you?'

175

'Fine,' she said, slightly groggy.

'The nurses tell me you gained four pounds since the last time I saw you. That's just terrific,' he said, and smiled at Frances and Oswald. Then he turned back to Patsy. 'In just a little while we're going to take you down the hall to another room and work on your leg a bit, but you won't feel a thing and when you wake up everybody will be right here waiting for you.'

He picked up the photograph of Patsy and Jack from her bedside table. 'Is this the bird you were telling me about?'

'Yes, sir,' she said, smiling sleepily.

'Well, he's a fine-looking fellow,' he said, patting her arm. 'And we are going to get you fixed up as good as new and back home again as fast as we can, OK?'

'OK.'

When Frances went out with Dr. Glickman to ask a few last-minute questions a woman came in with papers to sign and asked Oswald if he were the father. 'No,' he said.

'Grandfather?'

'No, just a friend. The lady you need to see is right down the hall.'

When Frances came back they went over the papers together and she signed on the line where it said LEGAL GUARDIAN, even though she was not legal. She had just perjured herself on an official document, but as she told Oswald, 'If I go to jail, I go to jail. At least Patsy's leg will be fixed.'

Oswald's admiration for Frances grew even more during the long hours they waited. He was as jumpy as a cat and could not sit still for a minute, so he walked up and down the hall. He wanted a drink so badly he was about to jump out of his skin. But he could not leave Frances. He wondered why the nurses don't give a shot to the people who are waiting for the operation to be over to calm them down?

While he paced, Frances sat quietly and prayed and waited.

⋆ ⋆ ⋆

Everybody in Lost River was waiting to hear as well.

That afternoon, around one-thirty, when Frances called from the hospital to report that the first operation was over, everybody was relieved to hear that Patsy, according to the doctor, came through it 'just fine.'

⋆ ⋆ ⋆

That night as they were on the elevator leaving the hospital, tired but happy, Frances said to Oswald, 'Thank heavens you were here with me. I don't think I could have gone through this alone.'

Oswald had been lucky enough to find a room at a YMCA just two blocks from the hospital, and Frances was able to stay with a cousin who lived in Atlanta. They wanted to make sure that someone was with Patsy every day, at least through the next two operations.

★ ★ ★

Back in Lost River, everyone was coming to realize just how much a part of their lives Jack had become. They had all gotten used to seeing him flying around, hearing him sing, and ring the bells on his plastic wheel. Everybody missed the bird more than they could have guessed. But the one most struck by just how much she missed him was Mildred. Mildred found out that she had loved Jack as much as anyone, but she had not known how much until he died. She had loved him all along but did not know how to express herself in any way other than complaining.

A week after he died she went in the store with her head hanging and said, 'Roy, I'm here to apologize and ask you to forgive me. I'm so ashamed of myself I just don't know what to do.'

'What for?' asked Roy.

'For being so mean to that poor little crippled bird, always fussing at him, telling him I was going to cook him.' She looked at Roy with tears running down her face. 'I don't know why I did it. I really liked him.'

Roy said, 'Oh, I know you did, Mildred, and so did he. He knew you didn't mean all those things.'

'Really?'

'Sure he did. That's why he was always pestering you.'

Mildred looked up. 'Do you think so?' she asked hopefully.

'Oh, I know so. No question about it. You see,

Mildred,' said Roy, handing her his handkerchief, 'old Jack was a master at judging people, much better than me. One time these two girls I had never seen before came in, and I tried to get Jack to do a few tricks for them, but as hard as I tried he wouldn't do anything. He just flew around, acting all agitated. And it really made me mad that he acted like that until later, when I found out that while I was busy talking to one girl, the other was back in the office robbing me blind.'

'Oh, no,' said Mildred.

'Yeah, they sure did, and Jack tried his best to warn me. He knew they were up to no good. You can fool me, but you couldn't fool him. I tell you, Mildred, it sure seems empty in here without him. I guess I got so used to having him around I never figured he'd go and die on me, but that's what life's about, isn't it; you get attached to something and then you lose it. Thank God Patsy is making it through those operations, or I don't know what we would do around here.'

Mildred went home feeling at least a bit better, but somehow the loss of Jack made her realize that she never wanted to lose another living thing without them knowing how she really felt. From then on, after every phone conversation with Frances she would add, 'Love you,' before she hung up.

179

At the Hospital

It had been an anxious few weeks, but everyone was relieved when Oswald and Frances came home with the good news that the last of the operations had gone well. Next would come the long and boring weeks that Patsy would have to spend in the hospital lying flat on her back in a body cast. From then on, every other weekend the Polka Dots would ride up to Atlanta and visit as a group.

Although he was anxious to get back and visit Patsy, Oswald rode up with them only once. Once was enough. Seated in a car full of women, squashed between his six-foot landlady and Sybil Underwood, having to listen to them talk nonstop all the way to Atlanta and back, was too much for him to bear. After that fateful trip he only went with Frances alone or hitched a ride with Butch. He also rode with Roy, who sometimes went on Sunday and came back Sunday night.

Everybody brought her games or picture books to try and keep Patsy occupied. Oswald always brought her little drawings that made her laugh, especially the one of him in the car with all the women. One day when the Polka Dots came to visit they were surprised to learn that a delegation from the Dotted Swiss had just been there and presented Patsy with a beautiful hand-sewn quilt for her bed, with GET WELL SOON appliquéd in the middle. Although they were pleased that the Dotted Swiss had come, Betty Kitchen examined the quilt and remarked, 'It just galls me to say it, girls, but look at those little stitches. They have us beat in needlework, hands down.' Dottie put on her glasses and looked more closely and had to agree. Mildred said, 'Maybe so, but you have to admit nobody can beat Frances's macaroni and cheese; we always have that, not to mention our floating island.'

'And,' added Sybil, 'I know we are not to blow our own horn, but don't forget the tomato aspic.' 'Ah,' they all said, nodding, and felt better about the whole thing. Patsy suddenly giggled in the bed. Frances walked over and squeezed her big toe with affection. 'What's so funny, young lady?'

'Tomato aspic,' she said, and giggled again.

Finally, the day came when the cast was removed. Now, according to the doctor, came the hardest part, the long months of therapy. The goal was to improve Patsy's range of motion more each day and eventually get her back up on her feet and walking. But walking again was not going to be easy. They had to change her gait completely from what it had been before and retrain all the muscles.

Her physical therapy nurse was a pretty, dark-eyed woman named Amelia Martinez, who was impressed with the way Patsy tried so hard and never complained through the long grueling hours of painful exercise. One day, when Patsy was in water therapy, Amelia pulled Frances aside. 'You know, Mrs. Cleverdon, she's the bravest little girl I have ever worked with. With all the pain we have had to put her through . . . well, let's put it this way. I've seen grown men cry over less. Dr. Glickman told me he'd never seen anybody improve so fast in all his life.' Then she smiled and waved at Patsy. 'That little girl wants to get better and go home.'

During Patsy's therapy everyone came to visit as often as they could, and when they were not able to be there in person, they all sent her cards and letters that Amelia would read to her. Amelia soon got to know everybody in Lost River by their letters. Each time Frances and Oswald came to visit they were pleased Patsy was doing so well, but still her first question was always, 'How is Jack?' and of course they always said, 'Just fine,' and felt terrible about it. But what else could they do? All that mattered now was that she was improving. Even though all the strengthening exercises she was put through each day were painful and exhausting, they were starting to work. She was now able to walk a few feet without support. As far as Patsy was concerned, each new step was just one step closer to getting home to see Jack.

ALONG THE RIVER

The Lost River
Community Association Newsletter

Fall is here, and it's hard to believe that old Father Time is in such a hurry. Seems like it was only yesterday when summer arrived, but 'tempus fugit,' as they say, and Thanksgiving is around the corner. And we have a lot to be thankful for in our community this year, as the news from Atlanta is still very positive and Patsy's therapy continues to go well. All good things come to those who wait, and we can hardly wait until our own Miss Patsy is back home again. Don't forget to start planning for potluck and get those pumpkin pies and turkeys ready to go!

— Dottie Nivens

The days passed and Patsy's future was looking brighter. Amelia continued to report that she was making great progress. Even Mildred seemed to be getting happier but as fate will sometimes do, it threw Mildred a curve in the form of a letter from her old lost love, Billy Jenkins, who wrote telling her that he was now a widower and would love to see her again. And, surprise of all surprises, Mildred told Frances she was going to drive up to Chattanooga and visit him. It was the last thing in the world Frances figured she would ever do, but as she so often said, with Mildred you never knew which way she was going to jump from one minute to the next.

She had left on Friday and it was already Tuesday, and Frances had not heard one word from her the entire time and didn't know what to think. Then, around four that afternoon, Mildred pulled into the driveway. She could hardly wait to see her sister. She threw open the front door and yelled, 'Frances, I'm back!'

The minute Frances saw her she knew something big had happened. There was a glow about Mildred as she stood there wearing a new lavender pants suit, and she looked younger and prettier than she had in years. With her face flushed with excitement, she exclaimed, 'I've got news!'

Frances felt her heart start to pound. 'Oh, dear, do I need to sit down?' she asked, then sat down anyway.

After she was seated, Mildred announced, 'Well, I saw him.'

'And . . . '

'And Frances, I am the luckiest woman alive!'

Frances put her hand up to her mouth. 'Oh, my God. I don't believe it, after all these years.'

'I don't believe it either. I have dodged a bullet. Thank the Good Lord that the idiot got cold feet and I didn't get stuck with him. The man is a perfect fool. What I ever saw in him is beyond me.'

'What?'

'You know what he wanted, don't you? He wanted a nurse and a cook and even had the nerve to ask me how big my house was and how

184

much money I was getting a month from Social Security. Then he showed me a picture of his six daughters, and Frances, that was the ugliest bunch of women I have ever seen. They all looked like him in bad dresses. When I saw that I thought to myself, I could have been looking at my own children. Then he wanted to know if I had enough room for his granddaughter, who is just out of drug rehab, and her four kids to come and live with us. They need a mother, he said.'

Frances was flabbergasted. 'Oh, my word. What did you say?'

'I said, 'Billy, you broke my heart and ruined my life, and you want me to take you back now that you are old and all worn out, move into my house, and have me cook and clean for six people?' I said, 'Well, you are going to have to look around some more to find that fool, because it's not going to be me.' And then I left.'

Frances said, 'Mildred, I hope you are not too upset. Maybe it was for the best that you saw him.'

'I'm not upset at all, I feel great.'

After Mildred left, Frances thought about how strange life had turned out for Mildred. At age fifty-one she was finally over Billy Jenkins once and for all. Now maybe, just maybe, she would be able to see how nice Oswald really was. Not only was he nice, he had talent. Maybe there was hope for the two of them after all. Frances had grown very fond of Oswald in the past weeks and could not think of anybody she would rather have as a brother-in-law. She immediately put on her thinking cap about how to help things along.

It wasn't meddling. Everybody needs a little help, she thought.

★ ★ ★

Frances was planning another dinner party for Oswald and Mildred as soon as she and Oswald got back from their next trip to Atlanta, but something much more important came up. When they went to visit, Amelia told Frances once more that she was very pleased with Patsy's progress; she was getting better every day. Then she said, 'But I know from experience when a child has something to look forward to it makes all the difference in the world, and all she talks about is going home to see her friend Jack.' Frances's heart sank when she heard that, and Oswald felt sick. Frances did not tell Amelia that the bird was dead, but it was just a matter of time before Patsy would be coming home and going into the store expecting to find Jack. When he had died so suddenly they had all been worried about how it would affect her before she had her operations. Now they had another dilemma on their hands.

When the two of them arrived home, a special meeting of the Polka Dots was called and Oswald was invited to attend, the second male ever to be invited. Frances felt he had earned the right if Patsy was going to be discussed.

Dottie spoke first. 'We can't let her come all the way home and then when she gets here tell her he's dead, we have to at least warn her or something.'

186

'Maybe we should just bite the bullet and go ahead and tell her the truth,' said Mildred.

'What truth?' asked Frances. 'That all the hard work she's been doing, thinking she was going to get to come home and see Jack, was for nothing?'

Betty said, 'Listen, she still has six more weeks of therapy left. Maybe if we tell her just a little something now to soften the blow, it won't be so hard on her.'

Mildred asked, 'How can you soften the blow, tell her he's sick?'

Oswald spoke up. 'No, we can't do that. I know Patsy and that would only worry her.'

'He's right,' said Frances.

After much discussion, they finally decided what they would do. A letter would be written as soon as possible and because of her literary background, Dottie would be the one to write it. And her nurse Amelia, the one Patsy liked so much, would be the one to read it out loud to her.

After it was finished, Butch got in his truck and drove it to Atlanta, hand-delivered it to Amelia Martinez, and then turned around and ran like a bandit. That afternoon after therapy, Amelia sat by Patsy's bed and read the letter out to her.'

Dear Patsy,

I am writing to you on behalf of all your friends here in Lost River to tell you the most wonderful news! Not more than a week after you left a man came into the store and took a look at Jack. As it turned out, the man was a top veterinarian who specialized in treating injured birds. After examining Jack, he told Roy he could fix that wing and he took Jack to his clinic and did just that, like your doctor did for you. When he came back you can imagine how happy we all were to see Jack flying around the store as good as new. We all wanted to wait until you came home so you could be there with us when we set him free, but the doctor said it was best to let him go now. After we knew he was nice and strong and had fully recovered, we all gathered at the store, and when Roy opened the door he flew straight to the very top of the big cedar tree across the street. And oh, Patsy, how we all wished you could have been there with us to see it! Jack looked so happy to be free and flying around way up in the sky, and to be back in nature again, among his friends. Just as happy as all of us here will be to have you back, among all your friends who love you. I know we will all miss not seeing Jack at the store anymore, but the other day Mrs. Underwood said she saw him looking fat and healthy sitting on a branch with a lady friend, so perhaps we may see a bunch of little Jacks flying around here in the near future. We all hope you will be home very soon and, just like Jack, be healthy, happy, and as good as new!

Best wishes from Dottie and all your friends at Lost River

Neither Sybil Underwood nor anyone else had spotted a redbird since Jack died, but Dottie said, 'I'll just have to believe the Good Lord will forgive me for lying just this once. And if He doesn't, then He's not half the man I thought He was.'

★　★　★

After Amelia read the letter to Patsy, she said, 'Well, that's good news, isn't it? Your little bird friend is all cured and well, just like you are going to be. Aren't you happy?' But Patsy did not look happy. She looked worried and upset. She remembered exactly what Roy had said about why Jack should not be outside and it scared her.

'Oh, Amelia, you don't think a hawk or an owl will get him, do you?' And then, for the first time since she had come to the hospital, she started to cry.

Amelia was alarmed. 'What's the matter?' she asked.

'I want to go home. I want to see Jack.'

★　★　★

A couple of weeks later Frances was in the kitchen when the phone rang.

'Mrs. Cleverdon, this is Dr. Glickman.'

'Yes, Doctor?'

'I'm afraid we've had a little setback here. I think you need to get to Atlanta as soon as possible.'

Frances and Oswald left Lost River at 5 A.M. the next morning and were sitting in Dr. Glickman's office by 11:30.

'What happened?' asked Frances.

'Well, the main problem is, she's not progressing. If anything she seems to be getting worse. We've done everything we can, but it's almost as if she's lost her will to get better, and without that, all the medicine and therapy in the world is not going to help.'

'Oh, no, what can we do?'

'At this point, for you people to spend what you are spending to keep her here is a waste, so I'm recommending that you take her home for a while, give her a rest.'

Oswald said, surprised, 'Is she ready to leave?'

'No, physically she is not ready; she needs much more therapy if she is going to improve beyond the point where she is today. I don't like to release a patient who is not fully healed, but in this case it seems Patsy no longer cares about improving . . . and she was doing so well. Do you have any idea what might have caused this?'

Frances looked at Oswald and then at the doctor. 'I think she's just heartbroken over that bird.'

'Are you talking about the bird in the picture she has?' asked the doctor.

Oswald said, 'Yes, it was a little crippled redbird.'

He brightened a little. 'Well, maybe a visit with him could cheer her up. We can try, at least. Is there any way we could get the bird here?'

'No,' said Oswald. 'That's the problem. The bird died.'

'Oh, I see,' said Dr. Glickman. 'And you told her?'

Frances said, 'No, we were afraid to tell her the truth so we lied and told her a veterinarian fixed him and he flew away. I wish we hadn't but we did.'

Oswald said, 'We didn't know what else to do.'

Dr. Glickman looked at the two distraught people across the desk. 'Don't be too hard on yourselves. At least for the time being she can still think he's alive somewhere. That's something for her to hang on to. Then maybe after some time passes she'll get over it and we can get her back up here and finish what we started.'

'How much time?' asked Frances.

Dr. Glickman shook his head. 'Not much, I'm afraid. My concern is that without continuing therapy the muscles will weaken, the leg will start to move back into the old position, and all our work will have been for nothing. Let's hope we can get her back right after Christmas.'

⋆   ⋆   ⋆

Patsy, looking thinner than the last time they saw her, was so excited when they told her she was going home she could hardly wait to leave. Amelia was sorry to see her go but helped get her packed up. As they wheeled her out to the car, Amelia waved goodbye and hoped Patsy would be back, but she wondered if she would ever see her again.

Patsy chattered happily to her picture of Jack all the way to Lost River, and Oswald and Frances both felt terrible.

When she got home she was still weak and could not walk very far. She had to stay inside most of the time. Everybody did everything they could to cheer her up, but all she wanted to do was look for Jack. Frances tried to reason with her. 'Darling, Jack is probably way off somewhere, busy with his own family, and he might not ever come back.'

But Patsy would not be convinced. 'Mr. Campbell says if you want something really really bad it will happen, and I want to see Jack really really bad.'

Patsy woke up each day thinking she would see him and was disappointed when she didn't, but she did not say so. On the days it rained, she sat in her room looking out the window hoping to get a glimpse of him. Frances could not tell her the truth. Dr. Glickman said it was good to have hope, even if it was only false hope. Christmas was coming and Frances was hoping for something as well: She was hoping that Christmas would be a distraction for Patsy and help get the bird off her mind once and for all. She told Mildred, 'This will be Patsy's first Christmas with us, and I don't care what anybody says, I'm going to spoil her to death.' Day after day Claude came up the river and delivered Christmas packages for Patsy sent from every store that had a catalog. Stuffed animals, books, games, and clothes arrived every day, and Mildred, who did some sewing occasionally, was busy making a dozen monkey-sock dolls for her bed.

Three days before Christmas, after the Mystery Tree had been decorated, Dottie called and said, 'Frances, I need to see you right away.' Frances walked into the post office and Dottie, looking grim, handed her a letter she had just pulled out of the letters-to-Santa-Claus box. Frances recognized the childish scrawl immediately.

Deer Santa Klause,

Please let me see Jack. I am sacred he is hurt. I do not want any presents. I have been a good girle I poromise. I am living at Mrs. Cleveaton's now. It is the blue hose by the post offiec.

Love your firend Patsy

The first Christmas Eve dinner at the community hall with her own child was not as happy as Frances had imagined. There was a pall on the entire evening. When Santa called her child up to receive her present it would not be the *one* thing she wanted most in the world. What was so heart-breaking for Frances and Oswald as well was that she wanted something that neither of them could give her.

Even the tree lighting that year was a bust. When Butch flipped the switch, there was a brief flare, a pop, and then nothing. When they left, Butch was still trying to fix it. But despite the tree fiasco, Patsy was cheerful on the way home. She didn't tell anyone, but she believed with all her heart that she was going to see Jack tomorrow and she could hardly wait. She fell asleep with his picture in her hand.

Another Christmas

Christmas morning, Patsy woke up early and came in the kitchen already dressed for the day, so excited that she told Frances, 'I'm going to see Jack today, I know I will!'

Frances winced. 'Now, honey, don't get your heart too set on it, you don't know that he's not off somewhere with his own family. Don't you want to open your presents? It's Christmas morning!'

'Can I do it later? After I've seen Jack?'

'But, sweetheart, you're supposed to open them on Christmas morning. If I had that many presents I just couldn't wait another minute. Mildred is coming up here to see you later. Besides, I don't think you're strong enough yet to be out all by yourself.' But Patsy was not listening, and as soon as she ate her breakfast she was out the door with her presents left unopened.

When Mildred arrived, Frances was alone in the living room looking upset and worried.

'Where's Patsy?'

'She's gone off looking for Jack. She left here an hour ago saying she was sure she was going to see him today.'

'Oh, no. Somebody's got to tell her the truth;

195

you can't let that little girl wander around all day thinking she's going to see that bird.'

'Well, if you want to break her heart on Christmas, go ahead. I can't. We should have done it sooner. But I just thought she'd get over it. Forget about him.'

Mildred went to the window and looked out. 'Ohh . . . there she is, over in Betty's backyard. I'll tell you, Frances, this is the worst Christmas I can ever remember. This is what we get for lying. I'll never do it again.' She turned around and looked at Frances with some alarm. 'If she ever finds out what we did she's going to grow up and hate us. She'll be scarred for life! Maybe she'll turn out to be a criminal. She could flip out and come back someday and murder us all in our beds for this, and it will be all our fault.'

'Oh, for God's sake, Mildred, you've got to stop reading those trashy novels. Things are bad enough as it is without you making them worse.'

But even the day seemed sad. The sky was gloomy and overcast. The usual Christmas blue skies and sunshine had deserted them.

★ ★ ★

Next door, Oswald sat in his room thinking about what an odd concept time was and how it never seemed to be just right. There was either too much of it or never enough. Before his doctor's prognosis, time had been just a round circle ticking on his wrist to check now and then, to see if he was late or early. Looking back on his life now, it seemed most of his time had been

196

spent waiting for something to happen. As a kid, waiting to be adopted. Waiting to grow up. Waiting to get over some cold or for some broken bone to heal. Waiting to meet the right girl, find the right profession, find a little happiness, some reason to live, until his time was up. Now the waiting was over and he had never found one thing he had been looking for until he found painting, and it had come too late. Somebody had sure handed him the short stick in life. And this year, probably his last, Patsy, just as he had, was also waiting for something that was never going to happen. He had watched her from his window walking around in the yard, looking for a dead bird she was never going to see, and it made him mad. This kid was going to have her heart broken. He was one thing, he was tough, but she didn't deserve it. He sat looking at the painting he had worked on all year, of Patsy and Jack on their birthday. He had wanted to give it to her for Christmas, but again it was too late. She didn't want a picture, she wanted to see the real Jack, and he wanted to get drunk. He knew all the dangers of picking up that first drink but he didn't care. He couldn't bear the pain of having to watch Patsy grow up and realize that nothing is real. There is no God. No Santa Claus. No happy endings. Things die. Nothing lasts.

And there was not a damn thing he could do to spare her from any of it. Even if there had been a God, that morning he wanted to punch Him in His great big liar's nose.

★ ★ ★

That afternoon Oswald hitchhiked over to Lillian, walked into the VFW bar, and took a stool next to a man in a John Deere cap drinking a Budweiser. Sitting in the dark room full of cigarette smoke and the smell of stale beer and the sound of the jukebox playing bad music, he began to feel that old familiar feeling. He was back where he should be. He was finally home.

He motioned to the bartender. 'I'll have a Bud, and give my friend here one on me.'

The guy said, 'Well thanks, buddy. Merry Christmas.'

Oswald Campbell said, 'Merry Christmas to you too, buddy.'

★ ★ ★

Frances had waited all day for Patsy to come home. By four-thirty that afternoon, when it was just starting to get dark, she gave up waiting, went out to look for her, and finally found her in the woods behind the store. The store was closed on Christmas Day but with great effort, Patsy had somehow managed to make it all the way up there, thinking that this is where Jack might be.

'Honey, you need to come on home now. You're not strong enough yet to be out this long. It's turned chilly, and you don't even have a sweater on. You know the doctor doesn't want you to catch cold.'

But Patsy would not give up. She wanted to keep looking as long as there was even a little daylight left. 'Can't I stay out just a little bit longer? Please?'

Frances could not bear to make her come in. 'All right, just a little while. But put this on for me.' Frances took off her pink sweater, put it on Patsy, and buttoned it up. 'I want you home by dark. Do you hear me?'

'Yes, ma'am.'

'You still have your presents to open. Have you forgotten that?'

'No, ma'am.'

She looked so small and frail, standing there in the pink sweater down to her knees, that Frances almost burst into tears on the way home.

Mildred was right. This was the worst Christmas she had ever been through in her life.

About an hour later, Frances heard Patsy coming up the steps and greeted her at the door. She had turned on all the Christmas lights and had hot chocolate and cookies ready for her. 'Well, *here* you are. Santa Claus has left you a whole bunch of things, you better come in and see what they are. Won't that be fun?' Frances had hoped that the presents would cheer her up, and Patsy tried her best to act surprised and happy at each gift she opened. But Frances could see that nothing, not the dolls, the stuffed animals, the games, or the new clothes, could mask her disappointment. For Patsy, the thing that really mattered was that Christmas had come and was almost gone, and she had not seen Jack.

★   ★   ★

199

That evening, after Patsy was in bed, the phone rang. It was Betty Kitchen.

'How's Patsy doing?'

'Terrible I'm afraid.'

'Well, I figured as much. Is Mr. Campbell there?'

'No. I haven't seen him all day. Why?'

'He didn't come in for his Christmas dinner so I wondered if he was over there with you. You know it's not like him to miss a meal.'

A little after midnight, Oswald had finally passed out and fallen off the bar stool. It was 12:45 A.M. when Betty woke up to the sound of loud knocking. She came out of her closet, put on a robe, and went to the door. The good Samaritan in the John Deere cap had Oswald slung over his shoulder. He tipped his cap and said, 'Sorry to disturb you, ma'am, but I'm afraid he's had a little too much Christmas cheer. Where do you want him?'

Betty had never seen Oswald take a drink before, but having dealt with many a drunk in her day she said, 'Bring him on in, no need to drag him upstairs tonight. Put him in my bed and I'll deal with him tomorrow.'

The man, who had obviously had a snootful of booze himself, walked into the closet and deposited Oswald on her bed. 'Merry Christmas, and to all a good night,' he said as he left. Betty took Oswald's shoes off, covered him up, and shut the door. She tiptoed upstairs, went into the spare bedroom down the hall, and got in bed, thinking to herself that this had been the worst Christmas she ever remembered. Patsy had had her heart broken, her mother had eaten almost all the wax fruit out of the bowl on the dining room table, and now her boarder had come home dead drunk.

Good God, what next? she wondered.

★ ★ ★

Betty did not have much time before she found out. At around 5:45 A.M. the next morning the screaming started. Betty's mother, Miss Alma, was standing in the hall in her nightgown screaming for her daughter at the top of her lungs. 'Betty! Betty! Get up! Get up! My camellias are flying off the bushes. Help! Betty!'

Betty woke up and heard her mother carrying on out in the hall, but she was so tired — she had not slept well — so she lay there hoping her mother would give up and wander back to bed. But no luck. The old lady continued to run back and forth in and out of her room, yelling about her camellias. Finally poor Betty got up, went down the hall, and tried to calm her mother down. 'OK, Mother, it's all right. Go back to bed. There's nothing wrong, you just had a bad dream.'

But the old lady would not be calmed. She grabbed Betty by the wrist and pulled her to her room and pointed out the window and screamed, 'Look! Look, there they go! Go get them!'

Betty sighed. 'Come on, Mother, calm down, you are going to wake Mr. Campbell. Let's just get back in bed.'

Miss Alma continued to point out the window. 'Look, look, look!' she said, jumping up and down.

'OK, Mother,' Betty said, and, just to appease her, walked over and looked out and could hardly believe what she saw. At almost exactly the same time in the house next door, Patsy sat up in bed and screamed for Frances. 'Mrs. Cleverdon! Mrs. Cleverdon!'

Her screaming startled Frances and she came running to the room. When she opened the door she saw Patsy, her eyes wide with excitement, jumping up and down at the open window. 'I saw him, I just saw Jack! He was here! I knew he would come!'

'Where did you see him?'

'Here. He landed right here on my windowsill and blinked at me. I know it was him. He came back!'

Frances went over and looked out the window and she too could not believe what she saw. It almost took her breath away. Although it was just beginning to get light outside, she could see that the entire yard and all the trees *were completely covered with snow!*

Everywhere she looked, for as far as she could see, was absolutely white, until all of a sudden she saw a flash of a powerful, incredible red streak by the window, then two, then four. When she leaned out and looked down, she saw that the ground was filled with big red camellias that must have fallen off the bushes. It was not until she saw one fly away that she realized that the whole yard was alive with redbirds!

By this time Betty Kitchen was running down the stairs, her large arms flailing in the air, yelling, 'Oh my God, oh my God, oh my God, get up, Mr. Campbell!'

Oswald opened his eyes and sat up in the small dark closet, and immediately hit his head on a shelf. He didn't know where he was or how he got there and with all the yelling and screaming he was not sure if he had died and gone to hell or what. Just then Betty jerked the closet door open and yelled, 'It's *snowing!*'

Pretty soon, people up and down the street were out in their yards, in various stages of undress, screaming and hollering, jumping up and down, and pointing at all the redbirds that continued to swarm up and down the street. There were hundreds of redbirds, in flocks of twenty or thirty, sitting in trees and flying around the bushes. With his head ringing with pain from a hangover and having just hit his head, Oswald struggled to get his shoes back on. When he finally walked out he was further startled. He had walked out of a pitch-black closet into a blindingly white world just in time to see a flock of redbirds fly by.

What a sight. It was still snowing big soft white flakes, and as he stood in the street it was as if he were standing inside one of those paperweights that had just been turned upside down. He didn't know if he was still drunk or not but he suddenly felt like he was inside a picture of some fairyland that could have been an illustration for a children's book. The Spanish moss, now covered with snow, looked like long white beards hanging down from the trees. As soon as she saw Oswald, Patsy went up to him and took his hand and — with her face flushed and her eyes shining — said, 'I *saw* him, Mr. Campbell. He came back just like you said he would if I wished hard enough. He came right to my window and blinked at me. Look,' she said, and pointed to the birds. 'There are all his friends. I just knew he'd come back!'

He looked up as a flock landed in the tree above and shook snow down on the two of them.

At that moment Oswald was not sure if he had died and gone to heaven, but if by any chance he was still alive he swore to God he would never take another drink as long as he lived.

★　★　★

Oh, what a morning!

Betty ran in, called her friend Elizabeth Shivers over in Lillian, and said excitedly, 'Can you believe it? Have you ever seen anything like it in your life?'

'What?' she said.

'The snow, look out the window! And we're full of redbirds. Are you?'

Elizabeth, who had been asleep, looked out the window and said, 'Betty, there's no snow over here. What redbirds?'

★　★　★

In the meantime, the Creoles had heard the screaming all the way across the river and wondered what was happening. When they came out and looked, they saw that it was snowing on the other side. As they all stood on the docks, the Creole children who had never seen snow were having a fit to go see it up close. And finally even the adults could not resist, and they did something they had not done in nineteen years. The snow was still falling as one by one, they all got in their boats and started rowing across the river to join the people on the other side. Pretty soon the entire street was filled with Creole men, women, and children who had joined their neighbors laughing and dancing in the snow. In less than an hour, word had spread by phone and the entire place was packed with people who had come from all around to see the snow and the redbirds. For most of the children who came, this was the first snow they had ever seen, and for the adults, it was certainly the first time they had ever seen snow in Lost River. But nobody there that morning, child or adult, had ever seen that many redbirds.

Frances and Sybil and Dottie went down and opened up the community hall and made coffee and hot chocolate for everyone, and when they switched on the interior lights the Christmas tree outside suddenly lit up. It was almost like Christmas Day all over again. Even though it was Sunday, Roy opened the store in honor of the snow and gave away candy to the kids and free beer to the adults. He was busy opening a can for Mildred, who had joined the party, when he looked up and saw Julian LaPonde standing outside looking in. As soon as the others saw him, a hush came over the store. They all held their breaths, wondering what was going to happen next. The two men looked at each other, neither moving. Then Roy walked over and held the door open and said, 'Come on in, Julian, let me buy you a beer.' He knew how proud a man Julian was and how hard it must have been for him to come that far. To the astonishment of everyone, Julian walked in and took the beer.

Later, Oswald walked down to the river and watched the pelicans and the ducks and the egrets try and figure out what all the white stuff on the river was. Three pelicans skidded off the top of a piling and fell into the water and were mad about it and Oswald had a good laugh.

As the morning went on and the sun came out, the snow began to melt, but not before three people who had no idea how to drive in it slid into one another. A lot of strange and unusual things happened that day. Oswald in his excitement had forgotten about his condition and against the doctor's orders was out in the snow all morning. But he did not catch pneumonia and die; he didn't even catch a cold. But the best thing by far was that Patsy got her wish. She had seen her friend Jack again.

★ ★ ★

Naturally, after that day there were many questions. Why had it snowed in just that area? Why had so many redbirds come? Why had that one bird blinked at Patsy? Of course no one person could be 100 percent sure what had really happened that morning, but Mildred had a theory. She went over to her sister's house, stood in the middle of the living room with her hand on her hip, and declared with defiance, 'Frances, I believe her. I believe she *did* see Jack.'

'But Mildred, how could she? We both know he's been dead for months.'

'I don't care,' Mildred said, 'I think she saw him, I don't know how or why, but she did.' Then Mildred looked her sister right in the eye as serious as a heart attack and said, 'Frances, I think it was a miracle of some kind.'

Frances thought about it. 'Well, I don't know what it was, if she really saw Jack or if she just thinks she did. But I'm not going to question it. She's eating again, and that's all I care about.'

★ ★ ★

Of course, if the exact same event had taken place on Christmas morning instead of the day after, many more people might have believed a miracle had occurred. Still, everyone had his or her own personal explanation as to why it had happened. As far as Patsy was concerned, it was Santa Claus who caused it; he had just been a day late. And according to all the meteorologists, there was a perfectly good scientific reason for the sudden snow. A cold snap from the East swept down from Canada and dipped all the way down to northern Florida, causing the temperature to drop to 38 degrees, and the moisture of the river may have caused snow to fall only in and around the river area. The bird experts who appeared explained it away saying that the Northern Cardinal has been known to flock together in large numbers in cold weather; and not being a migratory bird, they most probably had been in the area all along, hidden among the thick foliage. However, Roy and Butch believed it was the fifty pounds of sunflower seeds they had spread all around in the dead of night on Christmas Eve trying to attract a redbird for Patsy that caused them to come. Roy had said if there was a redbird out there within a hundred miles that liked sunflower seeds as much as Jack, they might have a chance. But as to *why* that particular redbird had landed on Patsy's windowsill and blinked at her was a question for which nobody really had an answer.

As time passed, even more strange and unusual things started to happen. The night after Roy had rowed across the river to Julian LaPonde's house with Jack, he had found out that Marie was divorced from her husband. And after being apart for so long, Marie and Roy were finally able to get back together again. With her two children, the confirmed bachelor of Lost River was soon going to become a family man.

★ ★ ★

But romance did not stop there. A few months after the redbird event, Frances Cleverdon made a surprise decision. One morning she marched over to Betty's house and said to Oswald,

'Listen. I never thought I'd want a new husband, but I'll have you, if you'll have me. Patsy needs a daddy. She likes you, and so do I.'

Oswald was stunned. But after she left he thought about it and realized that he absolutely adored everything about the woman, from her gravy boat collection right down to her pink kitchen. He had just been too dumb to see it before. The truth was, he would love to be married to her and be Patsy's daddy. But before he gave Frances his answer, Oswald decided he'd better go back to Chicago and see his doctor. It was only fair that she know what she was getting for a husband and for how long.

When he arrived in Chicago and called, he found out his doctor had died. However his son, Dr. Mark Obecheck III, had all Oswald's charts and agreed to see him the next day. After he examined him and came back in with the results, he looked at Oswald. 'Well, Mr. Campbell, I've got good news and bad news. What do you want to hear first?'

Oswald's heart sank. He had hoped against hope that it would all be good news. 'Let me have the bad news first, I guess,' he said.

'The bad news is you are no long eligible to receive your disability check.'

'What?'

'The good news is that those lungs of yours have cleared up quite a bit since your last checkup. You are doing great, Mr. Campbell. Keep up the good work.'

'Really? How long do I have?'

'How long do you want?' asked the doctor with a smile.

'Forever.'

'Well, Mr. Campbell, I can't promise that, but you can try.'

'Thanks, Doc. I'll do my best.'

Before he left, he called his ex-wife, Helen, and told her all the great news, and she was very happy for him.

On his way home to Frances and Patsy, Oswald felt like he was the luckiest man alive. And he owed it all to old Horace P. Dunlap and that faded old brochure. He was no longer an 'accidental visitor' in Lost River. He was now a permanent resident. And if that wasn't enough wonderful news, one day right after Oswald came back from Chicago, Miss Alma, Betty's mother, came downstairs and out of a clear blue sky announced, 'I think I'll do some baking today,' and started up again. Everyone was so thrilled with her fancy cakes and petits fours that eventually Betty Kitchen started her own bed and breakfast and bakery.

Patsy, content that Jack was alive and well, returned to the hospital and finished her therapy. Within a year she was walking without even a hint of a limp. However, Butch Mannich continued to drive to Atlanta every weekend, even after Patsy finished her therapy, and within six months two new dishes of tamales and enchiladas were permanently added to the community potluck dinner by his new bride, Amelia Martinez.

The most unexpected development involved

Mildred. On that morning after Christmas when Julian LaPonde had walked in the store, she thought he was the best-looking man she had ever seen. And when Julian, a widower, had spotted Mildred he had asked Roy, 'Who is that?'

After a whirlwind courtship, Mildred, now a platinum blonde, had run off with Julian, and they were now living in New Orleans, having a wonderful time.

Dottie Nivens remarked, 'That's what comes from reading all those racy books,' and sat down and started writing one of her own, which won a first novel award from the Romance Writers of America. At last she was a real Woman of Letters both professionally and at the post office.

★   ★   ★

Five years later, right before another Christmas, Oswald T. Campbell came in from a meeting at the county courthouse and informed Frances with a chuckle, 'Well, honey, it looks like we are not lost anymore. We've been found!'

On Christmas Eve a new sign was to be unveiled in front of the community hall that said:

WELCOME TO REDBIRD, ALABAMA
A Bird Sanctuary
Population 108

That night, when Butch switched on the Christmas tree lights and the new sign lit up, Oswald squeezed Frances's hand, and they both

211

smiled and waved at Patsy, who was standing over with all the other children.

Then Oswald leaned over and whispered to Frances, 'Isn't it amazing how one little bird changed so many lives?' And it was.

Epilogue

Although Oswald lost his medical pension, thanks to the wealthy clientele that patronized the art shop at the Grand Hotel his work was soon discovered and much to his surprise he became quite a well-known artist. But as successful as he became, everyone agrees that his best work hangs in the Redbird community hall, and people come from miles around just to see the portrait of Jack and Patsy on their birthday.

★   ★   ★

And as for Patsy, she is a now a veterinarian who specializes in the treatment of birds and has grown into a lovely young woman with children of her own. Sometimes when she walks down the street, especially around Christmastime, a redbird will fly by . . . and it always makes her smile.

We do hope that you have enjoyed reading this large print book.

Did you know that all of our titles are available for purchase?

We publish a wide range of high quality large print books including:
**Romances, Mysteries, Classics
General Fiction
Non Fiction and Westerns**

Special interest titles available in large print are:
**The Little Oxford Dictionary
Music Book
Song Book
Hymn Book
Service Book**

Also available from us courtesy of Oxford University Press:
**Young Readers' Dictionary
(large print edition)
Young Readers' Thesaurus
(large print edition)**

For further information or a free brochure, please contact us at:
**Ulverscroft Large Print Books Ltd.,
The Green, Bradgate Road, Anstey,
Leicester, LE7 7FU, England.
Tel:** (00 44) 0116 236 4325
Fax: (00 44) 0116 234 0205

Other titles published by
The House of Ulverscroft:

ANGRY HOUSEWIVES EATING BON BONS

Lorna Landvik

The women of Freesia Court, in small-town Minnesota, are convinced that there is nothing good coffee, delectable desserts, and a strong shoulder can't fix. Laughter is the glue that holds them together, the foundation of a book group they call AHEB — Angry Housewives Eating Bon Bons — an unofficial 'club' that becomes a lifeline through forty eventful years. The five women each have a story to tell. There's Faith, the newcomer, a lonely housewife who harbors a terrible secret; big, beautiful Audrey, the resident sex queen; Merit, shy and quiet, with the private hell of an abusive husband; Kari, a thoughtful, wise woman with a wonderful laugh; and finally, Slip, activist, adventurer, social changer, who looks trouble straight in the eye.

THE ORANGE GIRL

Jostein Gaarder

Georg Roed, aged fifteen, tells us that his father died eleven years ago when he was four. He had never expected to hear from his dad again, but now they are writing a book together, from the family home in Humleveien in present-day Oslo. Georg is writing now because his grandmother found a letter addressed to him in the lining of his old buggy. Georg's father had hidden it there as a 'letter to the future', which allows Georg to get to know him in a way he couldn't eleven years ago. The person who figures most in the letter is not actually Georg's father; it is the mysterious and beautiful Orange Girl, whose identity Georg tries to discover.